HISTORY
WHEN A (
A SECRET
DEFEND HER COUNTRY

WISHING SHELF BOOK REVIEW
United Kingdom

Highly recommended! This Young Adult historical novel is set in the US during World War Two. It follows the adventure of a seventeen-year-old girl called Jane who is determined to be a Sand Pounder. If you didn't know - nor did I - a Sand Pounder was a horseman who, during the war years, patrolled the coast watching for the enemy. But it's not so simple for Jane to serve her country as, to be a Sand Pounder, you must be male. What follows is a well-told story which is evenly paced and populated with strong and interesting characters.

The author is excellent at enveloping the reader in the historical setting without overwhelming them with too much descriptive prose. She's also excellent with speech and works hard to develop her characters, particularly Jane, as they try to solve the many problems facing them during the war years. It's worth noting, the plot strays into the Americans' attitude towards the Japanese and Japanese internment. This element of the plot I thought was well-handled and particularly interesting. Overall, this is a gripping read which I think most young adults, particularly those interested in the Second World War and the American's attitude towards Japanese after Pearl Harbor, will find of interest. The writing style is simple and flows well, and there's plenty to admire in Jane, the plucky protagonist. All in all, it's a bit of a gem!

MIDWEST BOOK REVIEW
Chicago

Young adult historical fiction readers will find *The Sand Pounder* an intriguing story. It follows a young equestrian who wants to join the U.S. Coast Guard-enlisted horsemen who patrolled the beaches of the West Coast on horseback to watch for an invasion by sea during World War II.

Like everyone around her, seventeen-year-old Jane is concerned about the war and its threat. Forced to grow up early when her parents both died of polio two years earlier, Jane and her brother Luke live in the family's home in the Tillamook Valley in Oregon. Though Hawaii seems very far away, Pearl Harbor's bombing brings the war too close to home. How can she help?

Jane would use her riding skills and her beloved horse Star to help patrol the beaches, but there's one problem—women and girls are not normally part of this kind of war effort. There's only one solution.

As Jane struggles with her new role and secret identity as John Morris, she must make many adjustments to support her new persona: "*Pushing down her natural response to express concern, Jane tried to respond as she felt a man would. "Whoa, cowboy! Is that how you were taught to ride?" Jane said as she ran over to him.*"

When she and fellow Sand Pounder Stephen Peters come upon a man who claims to be an American citizen escaped from a Japanese sub, their choices become even more complicated...as does their friendship, which moves from being comrades to an infatuation and something more, on Jane's part.

History comes to life, as do women's issues and roles during World War II, as Jane struggles with her revised role and its consequences.

M.J. Evans does an excellent job of winding the era's history and the lesser-known job of the

Sand Pounders into a realistic story of a mature teen's determination to make a difference in her world.

Black and white illustrations by Hasitha Eranga and Gaspar Sabater support the story with visuals peppered throughout.

Teens interested in realistic historical fiction that is fast-paced, well written, and character-driven by a strong young woman and her dual passion for horses and her country will find *The Sand Pounder* an inviting read.

The Sand Pounder

Love and Drama on Horseback in WWII

M.J. Evans

DANCING HORSE PRESS

M.J. Evans/Dancing Horse Press
7013 S. Telluride St., Foxfield, CO 80016
www.dancinghorsepress.com

Publishers Cataloging-In-Publication Data
Name: M.J. Evans, Author
Title: The Sand Pounder / M.J. Evans
Description: Foxfield, Colorado: Dancing Horse Press (2021)/ Interest, Age Level: 13 and up / Includes bibliographical references. / Summary: From 1942 to 1944, the U.S. Coast Guard fielded a mounted beach patrol along the coastlines to prevent an invasion during WWII. The call went out across the country to recruit horsemen to volunteer. A talented horsewoman, desiring to serve her country, answers the call, but must disguise herself as a man in order to join.
Subjects: Horses – United States—History – Young Adult – Historical Fiction – Horsemen and Horsewomen – World War II – Japanese Internment – 20th Century – Fiction -- U.S. Coast Guard

Ordering Information:
Quantity sales. Special discounts are available on quantity purchases by corporations, associations, and others. For details, contact the "Special Sales Department" at the address above.

The Sand Pounder/M.J. Evans -- 1st ed.
ISBN 978-1-7330204-8-0 (print)
Library of Congress Control Number: 2021914306

ON PATROL

From 1942 to 1944 during WWII, the United States Coast Guard Mounted Beach Patrol covered more than 3,700 miles of coastline on both coasts and employed about 24,000 men. Patrols on horseback worked in pairs, riding roughly a hundred feet apart, usually covering a two-mile stretch. They were called "Sand Pounders" and were able to cover difficult terrain quickly and efficiently.

This book is dedicated to those men and their wonderful horses.

The Sand Pounder

1

December 1941

Jane's hand trembled as she slowly twisted the knob on the old radio, trying to reduce the static interference and get better reception. She leaned forward, determined to catch every word of the president's speech.

"Yesterday, December 7ᵗʰ, 1941 — a date which will live in infamy — the United States of America was suddenly and deliberately attacked by naval and air forces of the Empire of Japan."

The teenage girl felt her stomach twist. Her unruly blond curls fell over her face as she leaned down. Jane swallowed as she continued to stare at the large wooden box with its cloth-covered speakers. With pounding heart, she strained to decipher every word. She listened to President Franklin D. Roosevelt inform the nation that the war so many had been trying to avoid had come to our shores with an attack on the naval base at Pearl Harbor in Hawaii.

The speech was short, just over seven minutes in length, but its impact would reach the entire world. Deep in her bones, Jane knew that her life was about to change.

Jane was a mature seventeen-year-old. She and her older brother, Luke, were forced to grow up quickly when both their parents died from polio almost two years earlier.

The home in which Jane and her brother now lived had been in the family since their grandparents came to the damp Tillamook Valley in 1894 with the famous Canadian cheesemaker, Peter McIntosh. Their grandfather, father, and now Luke, all worked at the Tillamook Cheese Factory, the pride of the town, producing what most people considered the world's best cheese. With the loss of their parents, Luke and Jane took care of one another, Luke working at the factory and Jane finishing school and caring for the house.

At the end of the president's speech, Jane turned away from the radio. Her brother was sitting on the edge of the couch, his elbows resting on his knees, his hands clutched, his head down. His hair was falling forward, covering his face.

Jane sat back on her heels. "Luke, what is he talking about? Where is Pearl Harbor and what do the Japanese have to do with anything? I know we have been collecting metal, but I thought we might get into the war with Germany. Where did Japan come from?"

Luke kept his head down as he shook it from side to side. "I don't know, Jane. This is as much a surprise to me as it is to you. I do know that Pearl Harbor is a naval base in Hawaii, but that's all I know."

"How close is Hawaii to us? Are we in danger, too?" Jane asked, her heart pounding.

"Oh, don't worry, Jane. Hawaii is a long way away," he said as he pushed his hair back from his face.

Jane couldn't help but notice the tension in his jaw as he stood and left the room.

The next day was a Tuesday and Jane spent it as she always did—going to classes at Tillamook High School. There was much nervous and excited chatter both in the hallways and in the classrooms about President Roosevelt's speech from the day before. Jane's history teacher, Mr. Johnson, spent the entire class talking about the attack on Pearl Harbor and why it happened.

"Yes, class," he said to quiet his students. "I know you have lots of questions and I shall try my best to answer them with the information available."

Jane was the first to raise her hand.

"Yes, Miss Morris?"

"Why did the Japanese attack us?" Jane said, her eyes glued to her instructor, pleading for a response that would comfort her.

"The answer is complicated," he said, "and actually goes back a couple of decades when our country started siding with the Chinese when Japan began invading China. We placed embargos on products that Japan needed, such as oil, steel, and iron – products that are vital to advancing their military agenda. Faced with serious shortages as a result of the embargo, and probably convinced that the U.S. officials opposed further negotiations, Japan's leaders must have come to the conclusion that they had to act swiftly. For their part, our leaders had not given up on a negotiated settlement and, I'm sure, doubted that Japan had the military strength to attack a distant U.S. territory such as Hawaii. Honolulu is almost four thousand miles from Tokyo. No doubt, they were as stunned as all of us when the unthinkable happened and Japanese planes bombed the U.S. fleet at Pearl Harbor just two days ago. As you know, we have now declared war with Japan and, since Japan has formed an alliance with Germany and Italy, I have no doubt that we are now facing war in both Europe and Asia."

A portentous silence filled the classroom. Jane's hands twisted in her lap. She glanced over at Jeannie, her long-time friend having shared a love of horses since grade school, and noticed her looking down, twisting her pencil.

Mr. Johnson looked around the room at his students as if he had never seen them sit in silence before. "Are there any other questions, students?" he asked.

Slowly, Jane raised her hand again.

Mr. Johnson acknowledged her with a nod of his head.

"Mr. Johnson, if we have to fight two wars at the same time, won't that mean we'll have to send a lot of soldiers and sailors into battle?"

Mr. Johnson pursed his lips before nodding. "Yes, Miss Morris. I'm afraid that is what it means."

Returning home from school, Jane set about doing her chores. She mixed up a meatloaf and placed it in the oven beside two baking potatoes from their own garden. As the food baked, she went out to the barn to feed her chestnut mare, Star. The horse munched on her grain contentedly as Jane mucked her stall, oblivious to the turmoil roiling inside Jane.

When Luke returned from the cheese factory, he was uncharacteristically quiet. He entered the house without giving Jane his usual greeting, washed his hands, and sat at the table. Jane brought in the meatloaf, potatoes, and green beans and set them down between the two of them.

Jane studied her brother's face as he ate. His sculpted jaw was tight. His dark eyes, hooded. Jane knew he was thinking about the war. "Our country is going to war," she whispered.

Luke stiffened and held his position, raising his head only slightly. Jane noticed the tears shimmering in his eyes. "Yes, Jane. We must defend our country."

"Why are you crying?"

"As much as it pains me, I must leave you and our home and join the Army or Navy to defend our country." A visible shiver went through Luke's tall, lean frame. He raked his fingers through his straight black hair.

Jane bolted out of her chair and ran to stand in front of Luke. "You don't have to go. You are the only support for our family." She clasped her hands, pleading.

Luke dropped his head. His response was little more than a whisper. "Don't you think I know that? Do you really think I want to go? But the world is at war and we can no longer stand idly by and let others try to stop the Germans and the Japanese. We must do our part. *I* must do *my* part."

"But what will *I* do? I'll be all alone," Jane said, feeling the tears well up in her eyes and the muscles in her throat constrict.

"Grandma and Aunt Molly are close by. They will look after you. And you have friends and neighbors who will check in on you . . . and you have Star."

At the mention of her horse, Jane spun around and bolted out the door. Through the cold drizzle, typical of the Oregon Coast winter, the teenager ran, slipping on the wet grass and slick mud of the well-worn path that led to the barn.

Her head over the stall door, Star's eyes seemed glued on Jane as the girl approached. The mare's ears were pricked forward, and she let out a soft, welcoming nicker.

Jane threw open the stall door and stepped inside. The horse stood quietly as Jane threw her arms around her horse's neck and pressed her face against it. She held onto her horse for several minutes, weaving her fingers through Star's mane to keep from collapsing. As her breathing slowed and the pounding of her heart calmed, she sniffed loudly and wiped the tears from her cheeks with the back of her hand.

"Oh Star, what are we going to do? What are we going to do?" She took a deep breath and reached for Star's brown leather halter. She placed it over the horse's muzzle and flipped the crown piece over her head. With the skill gained from years of practice, she buckled the strap to the check piece. Looking out at the misty rain, Jane led Star out of the stall. She tapped Star's near front leg. "Bow," she said. The little mare quickly dropped to one knee. Grabbing a chunk of mane, Jane swung her right leg up and over the mare's back. The horse stood up. With a cluck and a squeeze of both calves, Jane sent Star off in a canter with only the waning moon peeking between the clouds to light her way.

2

December 1941

Christmas 1941 was the second-worst Christmas in Jane's memory, the first being just last year – the year of her parents' passing. Not even the lovely decorations on her grandmother's tree, the aroma of the turkey in the oven, nor the brightly wrapped packages were able to lift her spirits. The Wednesday after President Roosevelt announced that the country was entering the war, Luke had driven the old family car from the coast to Portland. There he walked into the Navy recruiting office and, after waiting in a long line, signed up to join the war effort. He was to report for duty four days after Christmas.

Jane curled up on the end of her grandmother's green velvet sofa, tucking her legs under a plaid, wool blanket made in Pendleton,

Oregon. The sounds of Benny Goodman and his orchestra performing "Jingle Bells" bounced out of the brand-new zenith radio that sat in a place of honor in the corner. The strips of silver tinsel that Jane had helped place carefully, one by one, on the evergreen branches, sparkled. Finding no comfort in either the music or the decorations, Jane pulled the blanket up to her chin.

Jane's grandmother came in from the kitchen holding a transparent pink, glass punch cup filled with sweet-smelling eggnog made with eggs from Jane's chickens. "Jane, dear, look at the beautiful cup I got from the gas station when I filled up. I'm going to get a whole set for free—a new cup each time I fill up."

Jane glanced up and managed a smile. "That's pretty Grandma," she said with little enthusiasm.

"Here, I brought you this warm eggnog. It will help you feel better," Grandma Morris said, sitting beside Jane and extending the cup toward her.

Jane sighed and let the blanket drop to her lap. She took the dainty cup. Placing it to her lips, she took a sip. The thick, milky drink tasted sweet on her tongue but did little to sweeten her spirits.

Grandma Morris smiled at her granddaughter, her pale blue eyes reflecting the love she felt for this young girl who had already faced so much in her life. She stretched forth a veined, wrinkled hand and brushed a curly, golden lock from Jane's forehead. "I know this is hard, having Luke leave. But you will not be alone. Grandma and Aunt Molly are here. You could even come live with us if you want. We would like that."

Jane shook her head. "Thanks Grandma, but I can't leave Star. I need to take care of her."

At that moment Jane and Grandma Morris were startled by a loud bang. The front door burst open with a gust of wind and rain. Luke entered the room, his arms full of freshly chopped wood. Water dripped from his hair and clothing and puddled on the oak floor of the entry. Jane set the pink punch cup on the table, threw back the blanket and hurried over to shut the door.

"Whew. It's a nasty day out there," Luke said as he dropped the logs in front of the fireplace. "The wind is pushing the rain in all directions." He pulled off his wet jacket and hung it on the hook by the door.

"Thank you for chopping the wood," Grandma Morris said.

"I'll do more after dinner. I want to leave you well stocked for the winter," Luke said over his shoulder as he stacked a few logs on the cast iron grate in the brick fireplace. After stuffing wadded-up sheets of the Tillamook Herald newspaper beneath the grate, he lit a match and ignited the fire. Before long, the room was filled with comforting warmth and a soft, yellow glow.

"Let's open gifts," Grandma said as she jumped from the couch and headed toward the tree. "Aunt Molly, come out of that kitchen and join us," she called.

Aunt Molly, as she was lovingly known, stepped through the archway that led to the kitchen. She wiped her hands on her gingham apron which was decorated with wide rickrack. A broad smile accented by plump cheeks covered her face. "Is it time to open gifts?" she said, a twinkle in her eye as she sat down next to Jane on the couch.

Jane sighed and felt her heart sink in her chest. This wasn't the way Christmas was supposed to be. She wasn't supposed to feel like this. She loved these people. Why did she want to run from the room and keep on running until this all went away? Jane clenched her jaw and dropped her chin. She looked down at her hands rubbing the velvet fabric of the skirt of her new holiday dress her grandmother and aunt made for her.

A package landed in her lap with a plop. Startled, she looked up. Luke was standing in front of her, smiling. "I bought you something special to remember me by."

Tears welled up in Jane's eyes. "I don't need something to remember you. I can never forget you."

"I know. But I want you to have this."

Jane slowly untied the red yarn that held the colored paper on the present. The stiff paper seemed to open itself, revealing a lovely white Bible. Jane ran her fingertips over the rough surface of the leather cover. "It's beautiful," she said without looking up.

"Open it," Luke said.

The young girl lifted the front cover. Taped inside was a black and white picture, discolored with age, of Jane and Luke as children walking hand-in-hand across their farm. It was taken during a much happier time. Beneath the picture he had written the words:

"Whether you can see me or not, whether you can feel me or not, I'll always be beside you, holding your hand."

3

January 1942

The cold rain on the Oregon Coast reflected not only Jane's mood but seemingly everyone's mood in the community. Jane noticed it right away when she returned to Tillamook High School in the new year. As she walked past the Tillamook Cheesemaker's logo at the entrance to the school, there were no groups of students huddled together talking and laughing, excited to be together again after the long Christmas holiday. Instead, students and teachers alike walked down the halls, shoulders slumped, eyes downcast. Noticeable was the large number of junior and senior boys who were missing. Those already eighteen, and the ones who could get away with saying they were eighteen even if they weren't, had enlisted as Luke had. By the end of 1942, 3.9 million

Americans would enlist in the armed services, and by the end of 1943 that number would swell to 9.1 million. For now, the absence of the young men was becoming obvious even at little Tillamook High School. There were far more girls moving through the halls than boys.

Jane walked to her locker without speaking to anyone, and no one spoke to her. She spun the dial on her locker – 2, 12, 22 – and lifted the latch. Her stack of books was still there, just as she had left them two weeks before. Jane hung her coat on the hook. She pulled her U.S. History book from the bottom of the stack and plunked it on top of her notebook. Slamming the door shut with a metallic bang, she turned and joined the other students as they sifted into the classrooms that lined both sides of the hall. Jane walked into the yellow room with the new, green chalkboard across the front. She sat at her desk and looked around, counting the empty seats, symbols of the changed and damaged lives all around her.

Jane caught the eye of her riding buddy, Jeannie. She forced a smile, and her friend offered a strained smile back. Both Jeannie's brothers had joined the war effort over the vacation. Her younger brother was just a junior in high school but had lied about his age to get in the Army. Jane could see her own sadness and worry reflected on her friend's face.

Their history teacher, Mr. Johnson, walked into the room, stopped in front of the chalkboard, and turned to face the class. "Welcome back from Christmas vacation. I trust that, even with the new rules and restrictions we are all experiencing, you had a wonderful time with your families."

No one responded.

"Yes, well, I know this is hard on all of us," he said, adjusting his glasses on his nose. "Before we begin our lesson, I wanted to make an announcement. As you know, for the last year we have been in a competition with Forest Grove High School to assist in our country's preparations in case we were drawn into this war, which, as you know, we now have been. It has been our job to collect scrap metal, and Tillamook High School Cheesemakers have done a remarkable job answering this challenge. We have accumulated an enormous pile of old appliances, rolls of barbed wire, metal gates, and every spare scrap of aluminum foil we could find. When we left for Christmas vacation, we were far ahead of Forest Grove. However, I am sad to announce that, over the school break, some Forest Grove residents found an old lumber train locomotive on a section of abandoned track in the woods. This put them far ahead of us, as you can imagine."

A collective groan washed over the classroom. Jane kept her disappointment in check as she twirled her pencil between her fingers. She had donated several old pieces of farm equipment she found scattered around her property, remnants of the time when her grandfather had grown vegetables on the land she and Luke now owned.

"Yes. Yes. I understand your disappointment at not winning the competition. But let us expand our vision and realize what a great boon this is to our war effort. That was the ultimate purpose, after all."

After the final bell that marked the end of the day, Jane and Jeannie walked out the double doors at the front of the stately brick school. Placing their notebooks in their baskets, they hopped on their bikes and pushed off.

The high school, built in 1912, was on the south end of town on 12th street. Jeannie lived just a couple of blocks north of the school, near where Jane's grandmother and aunt lived on Grove Avenue. Often, Jane would ride her bike with Jeannie and check on her grandmother, but today she felt eager to get home to check on Star. The misty rain seemed to be subsiding and she thought she might be able to get in a ride before the darkness of the night sky made that impossible.

Jane bid Jeannie farewell and headed south down Main Street, the coast highway 101. As she peddled, she glanced at the all-too-familiar houses scattered on both sides of the road. Yet, with their cloth and cardboard-covered windows, the familiar had become ominous.

"Hey, Jane, wait up."

Jane recognized the voice of Thomas Kato, her neighbor, and stopped her bike. Thomas was a year behind her in school, but they had been friends all their lives.

"Hi, Thomas," she said.

"I haven't seen you around for a couple of weeks. Did you have a nice Christmas?" Thomas said, brushing his straight black hair out of his eyes.

"Not that great. Luke joined the Navy and left a couple of days after Christmas."

"Yeah. I heard," Thomas said, dropping his eyes. "Robert joined the Army.

They biked the rest of the way down 101 in silence until they reached the Katos' house. "You know you can count on us if you need anything. It must be awful lonely at your house," Thomas said as he turned his bike up the drive.

"Thanks, Thomas. I know I can."

At the Katos' house, Jane turned right. She had known the Kato family all her life. They were a second-generation Japanese family. Mr. Kato taught Jane the Japanese word "Nisei," which he said applied to them as second-generation Japanese Americans having been born in the U.S. He was proud of this and showed his pride by always flying the Stars and Stripes on a pole near his house. Mr. Kato owned a fish market in town. Mrs. Kato took care of their modest home and large family. Their oldest son, Robert, had enlisted in the Army at the same time Luke joined the Navy.

As Jane turned the corner, she saw Mrs. Kato pulling the last of the vegetables from her summer garden in the backyard. The small woman stood up, pressing on the small of her back, and stretched. She smiled brightly and waved at Jane as the girl biked past – another ritual Jane had come to expect.

"Hi Mrs. Kato," called Jane as she waved.

"Good day, young lady. Do you need some carrots for that horse of yours?"

Jane pressed her heels down, engaging the foot breaks on her Schwinn bicycle and smiled. "You know I would. Do you need some eggs?"

"Sure could use some if you have extra."

"With Luke gone, I always have extra. I'll tack up Star and ride her down with a few." Jane took the proffered carrots, shook off the loose dirt clinging to the long orange roots, and placed them on top of her books in the front basket of her bike. Stepping through her bike, she pushed off and continued toward home. She smiled as she thought about her next task: riding Star back down the road with a basket of eggs for the Katos. She was glad she had the chicken coop. Her six chickens produced several eggs a day and she felt good being able to share with her neighbors. Eggs were one of the items that were becoming scarce as the government took from the large egg producers what was needed to feed the rapidly growing number of soldiers and sailors. Posters were appearing in store fronts touting the benefits of powdered eggs. Jane cringed as she thought of it. They sounded terrible.

Life all around her was changing faster than she ever would have imagined just one month earlier when she heard President Roosevelt speak. And it was not just the absence of Luke. Several essential items were now being rationed to provide for the war effort. Tires and gasoline were some of the first necessities the people of Tillamook were having to use less of. By April 1942, all households were limited to just a half pound of sugar – the first food item to be rationed. That was half of what the normal family would use, but more than Jane needed. So, she frequently shared her sugar coupons with the Katos on the corner, and the Olsons who lived across from her.

Jane's tires swerved on the mud as she turned into the dirt drive that led to her house. Star nickered from the pasture as she rode up. Jane smiled. A warm feeling coursed through her body. Some things hadn't changed . . . thankfully.

Jane leaned her bike against the side of the house and plucked the carrots from the front basket. "Mrs. Kato sent you a present, girl," Jane said as she walked to the fence. Star's beautiful chestnut head with the white star right in the middle of her forehead, hung over the top rail in anticipation. The mare knew the routine as well as Jane did. First, Jane rubbed the carrot through the long, wet grass to clean it. Then she broke it into chunks. One at a time, she offered the carrot pieces to Star in her flattened hand, thumb tucked to the side. Star reached over the fence and, with gentle, searching lips, took the carrot from her palm. This was repeated until the carrot was gone and Stars eyes smiled with contentment. Once she fed all the carrots to Star, Jane returned to the house to put on her riding breeches, boots, and a warm jacket.

Jane walked to the barn with Star following along on the other side of the fence. She pushed the center barn door open and stepped into her favorite spot. She breathed deeply of the scent of hay and leather, the floating dust particles causing her to sneeze. Star came into her stall. "Let's go for a ride, girl. What do ya say?"

Jane clipped on the halter and led her horse out of the stall. She put her in the cross ties that spanned the width of the barn aisle by attaching a clip to each side of the mare's halter. Reaching into her grooming box, she pulled out a curry comb and a brush. "Here we go, girl. Let's get you all clean and beautiful," she said as she began currying and brushing Star's chestnut red coat. Her final grooming job was to pick the sticky, Oregon mud from the mare's hooves.

Jane hummed as she placed her English pad and saddle on Star's back. Her friend Jeannie used a heavy, western saddle on her sturdy quarter horse, but Jane preferred the lighter, smaller

English saddle. She felt a closer connection to her horse in that saddle.

After buckling the girth and pulling the stirrups down the leathers, she reached for her snaffle bridle. She placed the reins over her horse's neck as Star lowered her head. Jane released the halter and slipped the gentle bit into Star's mouth and the headstall over her ears.

"Wait here while I gather some eggs for the Katos," she said, patting the mare on the neck. Grabbing a canvas bag, she gathered a half dozen eggs from the stall that doubled as a chicken coop.

The ride down the road to the Katos' house was made pleasant by the fact that the misty rain subsided and the clouds parted just enough to let the sun peek through. Jane kept Star at a walk so as not to jostle the eggs. Reaching the Katos' front gate, she dismounted and led the horse up to the front door, the reins in one hand and the canvas bag in the other. As she stepped up on the porch, the front door flew open and two of the Kato children greeted her with bright smiles and sparkling eyes. "We have some *senbei* for you," said Patti, the oldest girl in the family, as she took the eggs. "Wait right here."

Patti soon returned with the rice crackers, a favorite Japanese snack, tucked in Jane's canvas bag and another carrot for Star.

"Make her bow," Paul, Patti's little brother said, clapping his hands as Thomas joined his two younger siblings at the door.

Jane tapped Star's left front leg and Star obediently lowered herself until her knee rested on the ground. Jane tucked her left foot in the stirrup, swung her right leg over Star's lowered back, and settled into the saddle as Star stood up. "See you again soon. Thanks for the *senbei*," Jane said as she waved and turned Star around.

She rode out the gate and back down the road. When Jane arrived at her house, she reached down from the saddle and hooked the canvas bag holding the *senbei* on the mailbox. Her hands now free, she headed for the beach along Tillamook Bay at a brisk trot. She posted, up and down in rhythm with her horse's two-beat trot. Once they reached the firm, wet sand, she asked Star for a canter. She sat in the saddle, letting her hips move with the swinging motion of the horse's long strides. Her shoulder length hair flowed back away from her face and the salty air filled her lungs. For a time, her worries evaporated and were replaced with pure joy.

When Jane returned to her home, her neighbors from across the street were waiting for her. Their faces seemed unusually stern and Jane, unsure how to read their expressions, felt her heart pounding and her body tense. She dismounted quickly. "Mr. and Mrs. Olson," she said. "Is something wrong?"

Mrs. Olson looked down and twisted the corner of her sweater. Mr. Olson cleared his throat then began to speak. "We felt we needed to talk to you about something of grave importance," he began.

Jane bit her lip and rubbed her palms down the legs of her riding pants. She looked back and forth between these two neighbors she had known for several years. She had no idea where this was going, but she didn't like the sound of it.

"What is it?" she said, her voice little more than a whisper.

Setting his jaw, Mr. Olson hesitated. Mrs. Olson reached over and touched his arm, her eyes pleading. "I think it best if I just get right to the point," Mr. Olson began. "We have noticed how much time you spend with the Katos."

Jane scrunched her face in confusion. "The Katos? They're our neighbors. I always visit with them. Thomas and I are friends. Why?"

"Well . . . with the war and all . . ." Mrs. Olson began.

"The war? What does that have to do with the Katos?"

"They're *Japanese*, after all," said Mr. Olson, gruffly.

"They're *Americans*," responded Jane, crossing her arms over her chest, her eyes darting back and forth between the two.

"You can't be too sure where people's loyalties lie," Mr. Olson said.

"Well, I can. The Katos were born here. They have lived here all their lives. They love America. Haven't you noticed the flag they always fly?"

Jane felt perspiration rising on her forehead and she swiftly brushed it away. Frustrated and shocked, she added, "You know the Katos as well as I do. Why are you saying this?"

"There's been talk," said Mrs. Olson.

"The government may have to do something," added Mr. Olson.

"Like what?" asked Jane, her head cocked to one side, her eyebrows knotted.

"We don't know. But we need to protect our country. . . ourselves," said Mr. Olson, placing his fisted hands on his hips.

Mrs. Olson reached over and took Jane's hand. "We just wanted to warn you to be careful."

Jane jerked her hand away. "I don't need you to warn me about the Katos. They're just fine," Jane said, adding, "Please excuse me. I need to take care of Star." She turned on the heels of her riding boots and stomping to the barn, her horse following behind her. She felt badly that she had been so abrupt with her neighbors, but she felt confused and upset by their comments. How could they be suspicious of the Katos? They knew the Katos as well as she did. *Oh, relax,* she told herself. *This will all blow over soon.*

But it didn't blow over. In fact, it wasn't long before things became much worse.

4

January 1942

Just two weeks after the Olson's visit, Jane mounted Star for a Saturday morning ride in the rare January sunshine. She walked and trotted down the side of the road, heading toward Highway 101. As she approached the Katos' house, Star abruptly stopped, tossed her head, and snorted.

"What is it, Star?" Jane said as she stroked her mare's neck.

Star snorted again.

Jane looked over at the Katos' house. Mr. and Mrs. Kato and Thomas were cleaning up glass below their broken front window.

"Hi, Mr. and Mrs. Kato. Hi, Thomas," Jane called out.

The parents turned. Their faces appeared older than their ages, lined with wrinkles, and their mouths were turned down. Mr. Kato raised his hand slightly in acknowledgement.

Thomas turned abruptly toward her. His eyes were as dark as flint. His nostrils were flared, his lips curled back over his clenched teeth. Jane had never seen him look like that and it scared her.

Jane hopped down from her horse and led Star through the gate. "What happened to your window?" she asked.

Mrs. Kato burst into tears. Mr. Kato wrapped his arms around his wife and looked over at Jane. "Someone threw a brick through our window last night. There was a note wrapped around it," Thomas said with a sneer.

Jane gasped. "Wh-what did the note say?" she stammered.

Mrs. Kato buried her face in her hands as Mr. Kato hugged her more tightly.

"It said, 'Go back where you came from,'" Thomas said.

"Where you came from?" Jane said. "But you have always lived here."

"Yes. That is true. But there is a lot of fear in the hearts of people. Ever since the attack on Pearl Harbor, all Japanese are suspected of cavorting with the enemy, even those of us who are life-long citizens," Mr. Kato said as he continued to comfort his wife.

"Well, that's not fair and not right," said Jane as she stepped up to the couple and wrapped her arms around them. Her thoughts went to the

Olsons and the things they said to her a couple of weeks before. *Surely they wouldn't have done anything like this . . . would they?* she thought. Jane stayed a while and worked beside Thomas picking up the glass. "I'm so sorry this happened," she said to Thomas. "I don't understand it."

Thomas stopped and turned toward her, his dark eyes boring into hers. "I do. We're Japanese. That's all that matters anymore. People have even stopped coming to Dad's fish market."

A feeling of foreboding surrounded Jane as she mounted Star and continued her ride toward the barn where Jeannie was waiting for her. Star seemed to feel her distress. She stopped several times and turned her head to look back at Jane, as if to ask what was wrong. Each time, Jane took a deep breath and let it out with a huff as she gave Star a pat on the neck.

Jane's worries about the war, her brother, and the Katos melted away as she and Jeannie rode their horses along the beach, trotting and cantering on the wet sand.

"I'll race you to the rock," Jeannie said as she rode beside Jane on her black-and-white paint quarter horse.

That was all it took. Off the two riders and their horses went, kicking up sand behind them. Jane kept her eyes looking straight ahead between Star's ears, ignoring Jeannie's taunts. "Is that all Star has? Can't you go faster?"

Reaching the large sea stack rising from the ocean first, Jane turned Star in a wide, sweeping circle toward the soft sand. Star slowed to a trot, then a walk, huffing and puffing with excitement. Racing another horse was like racing the wind — hard to describe and harder still to resist. Jane laughed loudly. "You still can't beat us," Jane said as Jeannie trotted over to her.

A humming sound reached their ears and both girls looked up. A large blimp floated through the air.

"It's from the hangers in town," Jeannie said. "They're on the lookout for Japanese submarines off the shore."

The joy Jane had felt just moments before evaporated in an instant and was replaced with the crushing sorrow and worry she had been carrying around in her heart.

It was late in the afternoon when Jane, heading home, rode past the Katos' house. The window was now boarded up, making the entire house look deserted and dejected. Jane felt her heart sink.

Things continued to get more and more difficult for the Katos. Trips into town for groceries became challenging as the couple and their children had to endure the stares and hecklings of people they once thought of as friends. Oregonians, like the rest of the nation's citizenry, were starting to fear approaching food shortages. On January 30th of that year, President Franklin Delano Roosevelt signed into law the Emergency Price Control Act, which enabled the Office of Price Administration (OPA) to lay the groundwork for food rationing. People in Tillamook resented the Katos, seeing them as taking much needed resources that belonged to "real" Americans.

One morning, Jane returned to her house after feeding Star and the chickens to find Mr. Kato at her door. Hat in hand and head bowed, he said, "Miss Jane, I hate to bother you, but I don't know where else to turn."

"What is it, Mr. Kato?"

"Most of the store owners will no longer sell to us." He twisted the brim of his hat. "My wife and I need a few things and we are hoping you might be willing to pick them up for us."

Jane reached out and took the older man's hand. Looking into his eyes, she saw the desperation there. "Of course, I will. What do you need?"

Thus began a weekly trip into town to purchase supplies for the Katos. One particular day, she did her shopping after school then met her grandmother and aunt at the Fern Café, a cozy new restaurant on Main Street, for dinner. Jane carried her bags of groceries into the café and set them on the floor by her chair.

Her grandmother raised her eyebrows. "Seems like an awful lot of food for one skinny gal."

"Oh, it's not for me," Jane said as she settled into the cushioned metal chair. "I'm shopping for the Katos. Many of the store owners won't sell to them."

Aunt Molly's head jerked up and her eyes opened wide. "What? Why ever would they not?"

"Many people are afraid they might be helping the Japanese."

"Oh, poppycock," said her grandmother. "That is the most ridiculous thing I've ever heard. The Katos are fine people and loyal Americans," she said as she buttered a warm biscuit for which the restaurant was famous.

"You know that, and I know that," said Jane, brushing a wayward curl out of her face. "But not everyone knows that."

Fear of a Japanese invasion continued to rise not just in Oregon but up and down the entire West Coast. In the beginning of February, a nighttime curfew was placed upon the Katos and all other Japanese people living along the West Coast. If they were caught in violation, they would be arrested.

One night, darkness was settling in around Jane's little home. Her windows were covered with dark fabric and she studied her school lessons beneath a dim lamp. The wind and rain beat against her house, as though trying to find a way inside. Suddenly, the phone hanging on the kitchen wall began to ring. Startled, Jane jumped up and ran to answer it. "Hello?" she said, her voice quivering slightly.

"Miss Jane, it's Mr. Kato. Our baby is very sick — coughing violently. We are not allowed to go out after dark. I hate to ask this of you, especially with the weather so disagreeable, but might you be able to ride into town and pick up a bottle of aspirin and some cough medicine?"

Jane bundled up in her heaviest coat and rain boots. She hurried out to the barn, deciding that riding Star would be much faster than riding her bike. The sun had set, and the night was made even darker by the thick, heavy rain clouds dropping their load on the Oregon Coast. As she rode along the side of Highway 101, the headlights from rare passing cars gave her much appreciated visibility, but the water splashed on her and Star from puddles as the cars swooshed by. By the time she reached Ford's Drug Store and Soda Fountain, located in the first building in town to have an elevator, both she and her horse were soaked to the bone.

Jane trotted all the way back to the Katos'. Riding up to their porch, she dismounted. The door flew open and Thomas stood in the doorway, dimly backlit by the few lamps burning behind him. He stepped out on the porch, extending his hand and taking the brown bag from Jane. "You are soaking wet," he said. "Do you want to come in and get dried off?"

"Thanks, but no. I need to get Star home and take care of her."

"I understand. We can't thank you enough, Jane," Thomas said. "I'll always remember this."

Jane brushed aside his comment with a sweep of her hand and mounted Star. She hurried home. Putting Star in the barn, she took off the mare's tack and used a thick towel to dry her off. Before going back in the house, she threw the horse an extra flake of hay.

5

February 1942

February 19, 1942 became a major turning point in the lives of the Katos and all the Japanese-American citizens in the United States. Jane read the news the next day in the Tillamook Herald as she ate her breakfast of Kellogg's Corn Flakes. Her eyes skimmed over the article. Her heart beat faster and faster with each sentence. She learned that on February 19th, President Roosevelt signed Executive Order 9066. This order gave the U.S. military authority to exclude any persons from designated areas, especially along the West Coast. Although the word Japanese did not appear in the executive order, it was clear that only Japanese Americans were targeted. Jane dropped the paper on the table, spilling her bowl of cereal and soaking the newsprint with milk.

By April, national rationing of several food and household items was in full swing. Gasoline, butter, canned milk, and sugar were just a few of those necessities that the people of Tillamook were having to use less of.

By early May, the beauty of spring seemed to ignore the war. The air was warm, and the scent of flowers filled the air as Jane peddled down the road heading for school. She stopped abruptly when she arrived at the Katos' house. Mr. and Mrs. Kato, and their children were lugging suitcases out the door and to their old Ford station wagon. "Did anyone get the boxes of Jell-O and bags of rice off the kitchen table?" Mrs. Kato called out.

"I'll get them, Mother," said the oldest daughter after putting her suitcase on top of the car.

Jane dropped her bike and ran up to Mrs. Kato. "Mrs. Kato, what are you doing? Where are you going?"

The little woman turned and faced Jane, resignation written in her eyes. "We have been ordered by the War Relocation Authority to report to the control station located at the Pacific International Livestock Exposition Pavilion in Portland. We hear we'll be living in a horse stall until we are sent to a more permanent center in Tule Lake, California."

"NO! This can't be happening," Jane cried, throwing her arms around Mrs. Kato.

Mrs. Kato patted Jane's back, comforting the sobbing girl. "There, there. This too shall pass," she said. "My mother used to say '*Shikata ga nai*,' which means, 'It can't be helped.'"

Thomas stomped by, carrying a box of bedding. "It *can* be helped. The government shouldn't do this to us. We're citizens!"

At that moment Mr. Kato exited the house carrying a box that, based upon the grimace on his face, must have been quite heavy. Jane pulled away from Mrs. Kato's embrace and turned to face him. "Mr. Kato, please don't go," she pleaded.

He shook his head and sighed. "Sadly, it is not my choice but to obey what my government has ordered me to do."

"But it's wrong. You aren't the enemy."

"You know that, and I know that, but it appears that many others do not. They believe we, and all others of Japanese ancestry, are a danger and, therefore, they are convinced that what they are doing is right." He placed the box in the back of the car and turned to face Jane. "Before you can get people to commit atrocities, you must get them to believe absurdities."

Jane stood frozen in place, holding her bike, and feeling helpless. Just then, their daughter, Patti, stepped up to her holding a sleek, yellow cat. Struggling to hold back the tears, the young girl said, "We aren't allowed to bring our pets.

Would you take care of Sassy for me while we're gone?"

Jane's words caught in her throat. She just nodded as she took the cat from Patti's arms. Patti burst into tears and ran to the car, climbing in the back seat.

Jane stroked the cat's fur as she watched the rest of the family solemnly get in the car, wave goodbye, and take one last look at their house before driving away. Their sad faces were imprinted forever on Jane's heart.

The next day, Jane read a column in the newspaper written by the sportswriter, Henry McLemore.

"I am for the immediate removal of every Japanese on the West Coast to a point deep in the interior. I don't mean a nice part of the interior either. Herd 'em up, pack 'em off, and give them the inside room in the Badlands . . . Personally, I hate the Japanese. And that goes for all of them."

Jane dropped her head in her hands and wept. She vowed she would not let the blood-red blooms of hate that she saw sprouting all around her take root in her soul.

With the Katos gone, the house didn't stand empty for long. A new family with three young children soon moved in. Mr. Kato's fish market in town became a barbershop.

6

June 1942

While the seniors at Tillamook High School were recovering from their graduation celebrations, looking for jobs, and planting victory gardens, an ominous threat was lingering off the Oregon Coast. Deep beneath the gray, churning waves, a Japanese submarine named *I-25* and commanded by a veteran sailor named Meiji Tagami was watching and waiting for a chance to fulfill its orders. The submarine hovered offshore.

The commander and his crew of ninety-six were assigned to sink enemy ships as well as attack on land wherever feasible. Up until now, Meiji Tagami kept his sub far offshore to avoid being spotted by the blimps that came and went from Tillamook. His desired target was Fort

Stevens on the Oregon side of the mouth of the Columbia River.

Tagami took his time studying the routes the fishing boats took to enter and exit the mouth of the large river that separated Oregon and Washington. The commander was well aware that mines had been set to protect the waterway and he had no intention of falling victim to the deadly devices.

On the evening of June 21, 1942, Tagami initiated his attack. Bringing his sub near the mouth of the river, he surfaced. He ordered his gun crew to open fire on Fort Stevens Battery Russell. Fortunately, the wise Fort Commander realized the sub was out of range for their outdated armaments and ordered an immediate blackout. As a result, Tagami's shots missed their mark. Only one came close to the Fort while others landed in a baseball field and a swamp.

Regardless of the failure of the attack, the fear that ran through the community of Tillamook was lodged deep in every heart and seen on every face. The attack had taken place just sixty miles north of their erstwhile safe little community. Suddenly, no one in Tillamook, or, for that matter, *anyone* living along the West Coast of the United States, felt safe.

The already understaffed Army combined with the Coast Guard in a unique effort to patrol the beaches up and down the coast. Beach patrols had been undertaken since before World War I, but these were inefficient foot patrols and didn't cover much of the coastline. Something much more substantial was needed to prevent an invasion on the West Coast by the Japanese and on the East Coast by the Germans. The fears were not unfounded. In addition to the shelling of Fort Stevens, German Nazi spies were caught trying to get into the country from the beaches in both New York and Florida on June 13th, 1942.

With the shelling of Fort Stevens, the citizens on the West Coast realized they were not safe from an invasion. A call went out to horsemen to join a special group of volunteer servicemen. Radio announcements filled the airwaves, articles covered the front pages of newspapers, and posters were nailed to lampposts seeking recruits to a new branch of the Coast Guard. They were to be called "Sand Pounders." Their equipment would be provided by the Army and their uniforms would come from the Coast Guard.

Jockeys, cowboys, rodeo riders, show jumpers, and horse trainers quickly answered the call.

A few summer days after the call went out, Jane met up with Jeannie for a morning ride along the beach. "Did you hear about the new patrol called the Sand Pounders?" Jane asked.

"Yes! I'll bet there will be some cute horsemen going up and down our beach soon. Maybe we can both get a boyfriend," Jeannie said, fluttering her eyelashes.

"I want to join," Jane said, ignoring Jeannie's comment.

"What? You? In case you haven't noticed, you're a girl."

"So?"

"They only want men for the Sand Pounders. You can volunteer in the lookout towers, though," she added, in response to the disappointment clouding Jane's face.

"I don't want to be in the lookout tower," Jane said as she leaned forward and stroked Star's neck. "Star and I want to be Sand Pounders. I'm as good a rider as any man, and Star's the best horse anywhere."

Jeannie lifted her reins and brought her pinto to a halt. "Jane, it's much too dangerous. You might have to fight Japanese soldiers. Sure, you're a good rider . . . the best I've ever seen, but that's not enough." When Jane and her horse kept moving forward, Jeannie clucked and sent her horse off in a trot to catch up.

"Did you hear what I said?" Jeannie asked.

"I heard you. I just don't agree. I can handle anything that would come up. I know I can," said Jane, her eyes focused on the shoreline where the waves were crashing against the sandy beach. "I've even been practicing my target shooting."

That very afternoon, Jane made a call to the Coast Guard station. The station was located just ten miles north in Garibaldi.

"U.S. Coast Guard. How may I help you?" a woman said by way of greeting.

"I am calling to find out how to join the Sand Pounders," Jane responded.

The woman paused. "Pardon me for asking," she finally said, "but is this a girl I am speaking with?"

"Yes, ma'am."

"I'm sorry, dear, but we can only take men in the Sand Pounders. I appreciate your patriotism and loyalty to your country." Before Jane could respond, the woman added. "There are several ways you can help the war effort, however. Have you planted a victory garden, yet?"

The next day, Jane went to visit her grandmother and aunt. She entered the house to the sound of "Praise the Lord and Pass the Ammunition" by Kay Kyser coming from Grandma's cherished radio.

Grandma was sitting on her doily-covered rocking chair, darning socks — her service project for the army.

"Good morning, Jane," she said, her cheeks plump with a smile. "How are you doing?"

"Grandma, I need to talk to you about something important," Jane said as she sat on the couch across from her grandmother.

"Something important? What is it, dear?"

"I want to become a Sand Pounder."

Grandma cocked her head and pursed her lips. "A Sand Pounder? Do you mean the mounted patrol on the beaches?"

"Yes. But the Coast Guard won't let me because I'm a girl." Jane waited for a response as her grandmother looked down and continued darning.

Finally, Grandma stopped knitting and set her needles in her lap. She looked up and stared into Jane's eyes. Never one to beat around the bush she said, "I've never known that to stop you."

Jane jumped up and threw her arms around her grandmother's neck. "Thanks, Grandma," she said.

7

July 1942

T he next day, Jane rode Star to the stable
where Jeannie kept her horse, hoping to
find her friend. As expected, Jeannie had
her pinto in the cross ties, giving him a good
grooming. Her horse tossed his head and nickered
as Jane and Star approached. Jeannie set the hoof
she was cleaning gently on the ground and looked
up. She smiled.

"Let's ride in the forest," Jane suggested.

"You afraid the Japs might get you on the
beach?" Jeannie said, only half teasing.

Jane cringed at the derogatory nickname for
the Japanese and her thoughts shifted
immediately to the Katos. Her most recent letter
from Thomas was, even now, sitting unopened on
her kitchen counter. She couldn't explain to
herself why she had hesitated opening it. At that

moment, she vowed she would read it as soon as she returned home.

"No, I'm not," she said. "I just feel like riding in the forest today."

Jane felt her stomach tighten. She bit her lip, trying to calm her nerves. She could tell that Star felt her tension. Her chestnut horse was having a hard time standing still as they waited for Jeannie to tack up. A flood of relief flowed through Jane and into her horse once Jeannie was mounted and they rode through the stable yard. The two equestrians headed out on an old lumber road that ran along the back of the stable's property. The rhythmic movement of her horse brought peace to Jane's soul and she smiled. The warm, summer sun flickered between the tall evergreens that covered the foothills of the coast range. Jane drew in a large breath of fir-scented air. A brisk trot was all it took to give Jane the courage she needed to share her plan with her friend.

Bringing Star back to a walk, Jane turned toward Jeannie. "Jeannie, I have a plan."

"A plan? What sort of plan?" Jeannie said, her head cocked to one side, her eyes narrowed.

"You aren't going to like it."

"Are you still stuck on being a Sand Pounder?"

"Yes. And I need your help," Jane said, her eyes imploring.

Jeannie pulled her pinto to a halt and rested her hands on the saddle horn. "What do you want me to do?"

"I need you to help make me look like a boy."

Jeannie's eyes popped open and her eyebrows raised. "A boy? How could I ever do that? You're the prettiest girl I've ever seen? You could never look like a boy."

"I think if you would cut my hair and dye it brown, that's all I need."

"You're beautiful blond curls? Ohhhh," Jeannie moaned.

"It'll grow back," Jane said, fingering one of the strands hanging down from beneath her helmet.

"And your body . . . it isn't exactly, well . . . you know . . . *shaped* like a boy."

Jane blushed. "I thought of that, too. I'll just wrap my chest with an ace bandage."

"And what about your voice. It's too pretty," added Jeannie. "Oh, Jane, this is ridiculous. It will never work!" Jeannie said, throwing her hands in the air and startling her horse. "Easy Pinto," she said, recovering her position and stroking her horse's black and white neck.

Jane dropped her voice an octave. "I can do it, Jeannie. I know I can."

Jeannie looked askance at her friend then burst out laughing. Jane smiled, then joined in the laughter. It proved to be a great release from the tension she was feeling.

When Jane returned home, she spent several minutes untacking and brushing Star. Once finished, she turned the mare out in the pasture. Back in the barn, she mucked out Star's stall then retired to the tack room to clean her beloved jumping saddle and snaffle bridle. She rubbed the saddle soap into the leather, enjoying the sweet smell it left behind and the softness on the pommel and cantle of the saddle. The circular motion she used to rub the soap into the saddle helped her push aside the restlessness she was feeling. She was stalling and she knew it. In her mind's eye, she could envision the letter from Thomas Kato sitting on the kitchen counter.

Not finding any more chores to do, she finally said aloud, "It's time."

Kicking the stones in the driveway, she slowly made her way back to the house. As she reached the back porch, she placed her hand on the doorknob and glanced over her shoulder to the west. The sun was setting, leaving streaks of pink clouds over the Pacific Ocean. She could hear the distant waves crashing against the shore. A false sense of peace surrounded her.

Letting her shoulders droop, she pushed open the door and entered the kitchen. Walking past the kitchen table, her fingers glided across the square tablecloth with its blue striped, bell-shaped flowers at each corner. The tan-colored fabric was trimmed with short blue fringe. It had been a wedding gift to her parents. Other than some slight discoloration from years of use, the cloth was in excellent condition and she loved it. Her fingers left the tablecloth and folded into a tight fist as she turned to the counter and stared at the letter.

With jaw set and chin raised, Jane walked across the kitchen and snatched up the letter. She peeled open the envelope and removed the folded letter from inside. Standing in front of the counter, she was having a hard time figuring out her reticence. She had struggled with these feelings ever since the attack on Fort Stevens and the Japanese occupation of the Aleutian Islands off the coast of the U.S. territory of Alaska earlier in June—feelings of anger and resentment toward the Japanese. She tried not to direct her antipathy toward the Katos but found she wasn't always successful. *That's not rational*, she told herself. *You know the Katos and they are good people—they are Americans.*

Yet, with all the self-talk, here she stood, holding a letter she didn't want to read. *This is silly*, she thought. *Thomas is your friend. Just read the stupid letter.*

She clenched her jaw and unfolded the letter. After taking a deep breath, she started reading.

June 28, 1942

Dear Jane,

I was shocked to hear about the shelling of Fort Stevens. I'm glad that was not too near Tillamook. Even so, you must have been very frightened. Maybe you should consider moving in with your grandmother and aunt.

When that attack happened, we were still living in a horse stall at the Pacific International Exposition barns. However, right after that, we, and all the families here, were moved in old army buses down to Tule Lake. That is in California, just over the Oregon border from Klamath Falls. This camp just opened on May 27th to house internees (my dad won't let me call us "prisoners!"), but there are already more than 11,000 Japanese here and more are expected.

They only gave us a few hours' notice to gather our things before the buses arrived to pick us up. That was okay since we don't have much with us anyway. Most of our possessions were put in boxes and placed somewhere in storage by the army. We don't know where. My dad keeps reminding me that they are just "things" and not to worry about them. We have each other and that is all that matters. Deep inside I know he is right, but I still get angry sometimes.

We were told that we were being moved to an internment camp for our own safety. But when we arrived at Tule Lake after an awfully long bus ride, I was shocked to see a big, wire fence all around the compound. Worst of all, there were guard towers every few yards and the guards were pointing their guns at us! Why would they be pointed at us if they were trying to protect us? Is this an internment camp or a concentration camp? Or are they one and the same?

My father says we must behave ourselves and cooperate peacefully with whatever the government tells us to do. That way, we can prove that we are worthy of being American citizens. I must admit, I don't feel much like being cooperative, but I will obey my father as I trust in his wisdom.

I hope you are doing well, and that Luke is safe. We haven't heard from my brother since we were moved to Tule Lake. Our prayers are with him and all the soldiers. Please don't think poorly of me for complaining. I just never expected my life to go like this.

I hope to see you soon.
Sincerely,
Your friend,
Thomas Kato

8

August 1942

Over the next few days, Jane and Jeannie worked on the needed transformation. With a towel around Jane's shoulders, Jeannie cut her friend's blond locks. They fell to the floor in a soft pile around Jane's feet. Jane looked in the mirror. She felt her heart twist as she gazed at the strange face staring back at her. Then she nodded with renewed resolve. "Good job, Jeannie."

Setting the mirror down on the counter, she reached for a paper bag with "Ford's Drug Store" printed across the front. Jane pulled a bottle of hair dye out of the sack. "Now, let's color it."

Jeannie looked at the bottle. "Dark brown?" she said, her nose scrunching up. "Well, it'll be different."

With heads together, the two girls carefully read the directions. An hour later, Jane removed the stained towel and rubbed her fingers through her short hair. She shook her head, sending spray around the room. Jeannie screeched. "Don't get it on me!"

Jane grabbed the mirror. Gone were her golden locks, replaced now with short, dark brown curls clinging tightly to her scalp. "Perfect, Jeannie. It's perfect!"

"Well, I must say you don't look like Jane. Speaking of that . . . what name are you going to go by?"

"I thought 'John' would be easy to get used to," Jane said in her imitation of a man's voice.

"Good point," said Jeannie as she examined her handiwork from the front, the back, and on each side. "Yep. I did a great job. Maybe I should become a beautician."

Jane stared up at the ceiling of her bedroom, wishing the night would end. Every nerve in her body was tingling. She felt her heart pounding and she tried to slow her breathing and relax. Trying to talk herself into going to sleep was not working. She was too nervous about what the next day would bring.

At long last, the night that seemed it would never end relinquished itself to the early morning sun. The dark curtains covering Jane's bedroom windows refused to let the light in, but the clanging alarm beside her bed rudely announced the 6:00 a.m. wake-up call. Jane threw back her blankets and got up. Pulling on her jeans, Jane rushed out to the barn to feed Star.

Star nickered a welcome when Jane slid open the barn door. "Good morning, girl. Today is a big day for both of us," she said as she filled a scoop with sweet feed and poured it into Star's bucket. She followed this with a flake of grass hay and put it in the manger.

Jane hurried back to the house to ready herself. She breezed past the flyer taped to the pink International Harvester refrigerator she had picked up a few weeks earlier from the feed store.

SAND POUNDERS RECRUITMENT
RIDERS NEEDED TO JOIN THE
COAST GUARD MOUNTED PATROL
All experienced horsemen are
encouraged to report to
the Garibaldi Coast Guard
Headquarters at noon on
August 1, 1942.
Please consider volunteering for
this important mission.
Bringing your own horse is
desirable but not required.

The Garibaldi Coast Guard Headquarters was just ten miles away at the north end of Tillamook

Bay. She knew it would take her a couple of hours of trotting beside the road to reach the station by noon. And she didn't want Star to be worn out by the time she did reach the command center.

She grabbed a quick breakfast of corn flakes with canned peaches, then went to work on her appearance. A few days earlier, she had decided to use western tack and clothing to finish her disguise, deciding her English breeches and black velvet hard-hat looked more feminine than cowboy wear. Spread across the chair beside her bed were a pair of new denim jeans, a plaid, button-up shirt, cowboy boots, and a large cowboy hat. She had also splurged on a tooled leather belt with a shiny silver buckle.

Before putting on her shirt and jeans, Jane wrapped her chest with a long, thin, tensor bandage called an "ACE" bandage that she had purchased from Ford's. Pinning it securely with a safety pin, she examined herself in the mirror. Her body now looked appropriately void of curves. She smiled.

Fully dressed, she walked back to the barn where Star was still contentedly munching her hay. As was to be expected, the grain bucket had been licked clean. Jane led Star from her stall and clipped her into the cross ties. She brushed her copper-colored coat only briefly, having bathed her the day before.

Jane grunted as she threw the heavy western saddle on Star's back, missing her light

English saddle all the more. Star pinned her ears and glowered back at Jane. "Yeah, I know. You don't like it any more than I do," Jane said as she tightened the cinch. She put the new western bridle with its long-shanked bit into the mare's mouth and over her head.

Jane stepped back and admired her horse. "You look quite nice, Star," Jane said. The mare blew out a breath of air and pawed her left front hoof by way of complaint.

Jane and Star trotted along the side of Highway 101, the two-lane road that twists and turns the length of the Oregon coast. Once they reached Bay City, the road ran right along the edge of Tillamook Bay. The scent of fish wafted across the road and mingled with the smell of exhaust from the few delivery trucks making their rounds in the daylight hours, needing to be off the roads when darkness set in and curfew took effect.

Star seemed to sense the importance of the day and kept her ears pricked forward and her strides long and purposeful. In less than two hours, the mare had covered the ten miles from their home to the beach town of Garibaldi.

Jane brought Star back to a walk with a slight touch of the reins and a press of her seat into the saddle. Ahead of them was a magnificent, newly built structure in the Colonial Revival architectural style. Its roof was covered with red shingles. Green shutters

framed the pane-glass windows. The siding and
porch pillars were so white the entire structure
glistened in the sun. This was their
destination — the home of the U.S. Coast Guard
Headquarters on Tillamook Bay. Jane didn't
think she had ever seen such an impressive
building.

She dismounted and tied Star to a fence
post. Turning, she clenched her fists, dropped
her chin, and marched up the paved walkway.
She walked up the six, green-painted concrete
steps to the wide front porch. Crossing the
porch in three long strides, she stopped
abruptly in front of the door, her hand poised,
ready to knock. *Do I knock? Or just walk in?* she
wondered.

She didn't have to decide, for at that instant
the door was flung open from within and a
handsome young man, dressed in the formal
attire worn by show jumpers, stepped through
the door and stopped in front of her. Jane
noticed his neatly combed, wavy brown hair,
his sparkling eyes, and his strong, fit body. She
blushed and looked away.

"Hey, you here to join the Sand Pounders,
too?" he asked.

Jane's heart jumped to her throat and she
forced it back down with a swallow. She felt an
unfamiliar tingle course through her body.
"Ah, yes . . ." Her first attempt to respond came
out high and squeaky. Blushing, she cleared her

throat and tried again, dropping her voice. "Yes. Am I at the right place?"

"You sure are. I just signed up," he said. Looking over her head toward where Star was tied, he added, "Is that your horse? Looks like a beauty. I didn't dare bring any of my horses. They're all too valuable. Show jumpers you know."

"Oh . . . sure. I understand," Jane said, her voice steadier now. "That's Star. We go everywhere together."

"Well, the Coast Guard will be glad to have her. They're hard up for horses—waiting for a shipment from the army." He paused and looked her up and down. Jane felt the butterflies wiggle in her stomach and perspiration bead on her forehead. "You're not much bigger than the jockeys in there. You sure you can handle this?"

Jane puffed up her chest and lifted her chin. "Sure, I can. I can ride with the best of them. And I can handle a gun, too."

"Well, okay. . . if you say so. I'm Stephan Peters, by the way. Just took the train in from Boise, Idaho," he said, extending his hand.

"John Morris, from Tillamook, just down the road," Jane said. She wiped her damp hand on her jeans and took his outstretched hand. She shook it as firmly as she could. "Nice to meet you, Stephan."

9

August 1942

Jane scooted around Stephan and entered a large foyer. It smelled strongly of fresh floor polish. At the far end of the room a woman sat at a desk that was cluttered with papers and pencils. Around the room, young men, most of whom were dressed in riding attire, both western and English, were filling out forms.

Jane stepped up to the desk. The woman looked up and smiled. The eyes behind the black horn-rimmed glasses were green. The brown hair covering her head was overall short, practical, and curly, with a couple of waves to shape the front. The style favored the small, white, military uniform hat that was perched on top of her head. "May I help you?" she asked, her voice soft and pleasant.

Jane recognized the voice as that of the woman who had answered the phone when she had initially called. Jane cleared her throat again and consciously lowered her voice. "I have come to enlist as a Sand Pounder."

The woman cocked her head and examined Jane closely. Jane felt the perspiration return to her forehead and palms of her hands. She set her jaw and stared back.

The woman shrugged her shoulders and handed Jane a printed form and a pencil. "Please fill this out and return it to me. Do you have your own horse, or will you require us to provide you with one?"

"I have my own horse."

"Lovely."

Enlisting proved to be easier than Jane had anticipated. The form was quite simple. Name. Date of Birth. Home Address. Experience with horses. Experience with firearms. Name and contact of closest relative. She completed the form and returned it to the woman behind the desk. "We will have our orientation meeting with the Commander at 1200 hours sharp out on the parade grounds. Do you have your horse here?"

"Yes."

"Lovely. Bring him along."

"Her."

"Of course. Her. Bring her along."

Jane walked out the door to find several young men around Star.

"Great conformation," said one.

"Nice sturdy legs," said another. "I'll bet she's a hunter."

"Not in that western tack she's not," said one man in tan breeches and tall black boots.

Star stood quietly, allowing the men to fawn over her.

Jane stepped up to Star. Her horse greeted her with a nudge to her shoulder. The men chuckled.

"This must be your horse. She wouldn't give any of us the time of day," said a tall man in western wear.

Jane smiled and rubbed the star on her mare's face.

"What's her name?" asked a short man.

Probably a jockey, thought Jane.

"Star. Her name is Star," said Jane.

A loud bell clanged, and the recruits hurried over to the large, grass-covered field. The few that had their own horses led their mounts at a trot and lined up with the others. Jane brought Star to a halt next to a young man holding the reins of a palomino quarter horse.

All eyes turned to watch as a tall, handsome man strode across the field in front of them. Even Star watched him, her ears pricked forward. He stopped when he reached the center of the line, and turned to face them.

Jane guessed him to be in his forties. He appeared to be strong and fit. He was dressed in a double-breasted, navy blue coat over a white shirt and navy tie. The arms of the coat bore the Coast Guard insignia of an eagle above several gold stripes. His matching slacks were wrinkle-free with a crisp crease down the front. On his head he wore a white cap with a single band of lustrous, gold, oak-leaf ornamentation across the felt-covered visor. Mounted on the cap band was a gilt eagle, its wings spread, bearing a shield on its breast. The man was quite impressive, and Jane sucked in a quick breath in awe. Jane soon learned that this man was the commander of the base.

As the Commander was making his grand entrance, two Coast Guardsmen, dressed in navy jumpsuits with white caps, white belts and shiny black boots, were working their way down the line of recruits. They handed each young man a piece of paper. Jane took hers without taking her eyes off the Commander. It wasn't until he started speaking and was instructed to do so, that she looked at what she held.

"We will now recite in unison 'The Coast Guard Ethos,'" he said. Jane looked down and read aloud with the others.

The United States
Coast Guard Ethos

I am a Coast Guardsman.
I serve the people of the United States.
I will protect them.
I will defend them.
I will save them.
I am their shield.
For them I am Semper Paratus.
I live the Coast Guard core values.
I am proud to be a Coast Guardsman.
We are the United States Coast Guard.

Jane felt her heart swell with pride, and she smiled. She was proud to be an American. She was proud to be serving her country. And, despite the deceit, she was proud to be a Sand Pounder.

The Commander began speaking in a deep, yet mellow voice that Jane was drawn to immediately.

"You have just recited the Coast Guard Ethos. You will memorize it tonight. Welcome to all of you and a special welcome to the horses you have brought with you. I'm sorry there are not more but we will be receiving a shipment of horses from the army sometime tomorrow and each of you will be assigned an equine partner within a few days of their arrival. In the meantime, those with horses will work on mounted training, while the rest of you will train on the ground with weaponry."

Jane liked the sound of this, and she rubbed Star's neck.

The Commander continued. "Semper Paratus. That is our motto. It means 'Always Ready.' Among the many and varied activities of the Coast Guard during the war is the operation of a security force for the protection of our coasts and inland waterways. As a supplement to port security, a beach patrol organization is being established of which you have volunteered to be a part. Our shores are constantly at risk of being invaded by saboteurs and enemy attack. Our beach patrol is one of the most important phases of national defense. On June 13th, a foggy night, a lone twenty-one-year-old Seaman 2nd Class was making his patrol along the shores of Long Island. He came upon a group of Nazis coming ashore. This wise young man, though unarmed and without a mount, managed to run all the way to the Amagansett station to report what he had seen. Because of his quick thinking, the Nazis were apprehended, and disaster averted.

"We have been tasked with protecting American shores against sabotage, enemy submarines, and enemy landings. We have three basic functions: to detect and observe enemy vessels operating in coastal waters and to transmit information thus obtained to the appropriate Navy and Army commands, to report attempts of landing by the enemy and to assist in preventing such activity, and to prevent communication between persons on shore and the enemy at sea."

10

August 1942

Training began in earnest that very afternoon. The recruits who had their own horses went with the Commander. He stood in the middle of a field, his arms folded across his chest, as he watched them ride. He shouted instructions, and Jane, listening carefully, followed.

"Pick up the trot! Halt! Back up! Canter off! Halt! Circle to the right at a trot! Circle to the left at a canter!"

Jane and Star executed all the movements with ease. Out of the corner of her eye, Jane caught the Commander smiling as he watched her.

In the background, Jane became conscious of popping sounds coming from the shooting range. Star's ears twitched with each gunshot, but the mare didn't bolt or spook.

"Dismount," shouted the Commander.

Jane brought Star to a halt and swung her right leg over the back of the saddle, landing on the ground with both feet. She stood beside her horse and waited for the next instruction. Star stood beside her, breathing heavily.

The Commander bypassed the other riders and stepped up to Jane. "What is your name, Sand Pounder?"

"Ja . . ." Jane swallowed and felt a shiver run down her spine. "John Morris, Sir." She looked straight ahead, avoiding eye contact.

"Well, John Morris, I must say I'm impressed with your riding skills. Where did you learn to ride like that?" the Commander asked, his demeanor and posture softening.

"I've ridden all my life, sir," Jane said.

"We have a shipment of a dozen horses coming by horse van tomorrow. They've been bred and trained at Fort Robinson, an army facility in Nebraska. I would like you to meet the van and, after providing for their needs and assessing their overall health, begin working with them."

"Are the horses well-trained?" Jane asked.

"That's why I'm soliciting your help," he answered without hesitation. "I need you to ride and evaluate each one before I assign them to a Sand Pounder."

"Pardon me for questioning your judgment, sir, but aren't some of the other

Sand Pounders horse trainers?" Jane asked, looking now into the imposing man's blue eyes.

"Yes, some are. And all *claim* to be excellent riders. I would just like to know what I am getting. I'll expect a complete report on each horse from you forty-eight hours after their arrival. I want you to determine if the horses have adequate training, good health, and pleasing, or at least *workable,* temperaments. We don't have time to do a lot of reeducating, and I don't want to deal with a bunch of crazy jackasses."

"Yes, sir," Jane said, trying to show more confidence than she felt.

The Commander turned on the heel of his polished boot and walked away.

"Well, you sure impressed him," said the young man with the palomino.

Jane turned and looked at the rider for the first time. Typical of all equestrians, her attention had previously been reserved for evaluating the horse, overlooking the human. The young man appeared to be about her age though he was several inches taller. His pale skin was dotted with freckles and his green eyes were friendly and inviting. Jane shook her head. "I don't know why."

"Well, obviously, because you were the best rider out there," he said. The look on his face and the tone of his voice indicated that he was just a bit in awe.

Blushing, Jane turned away and stroked Star's face. "I just have a good horse," she whispered.

The loud bell clanged again, and all the new Sand Pounders lined up, facing the Commander.

"That was a good first day of training, men. I'm pleased with the effort you displayed. Pick up your uniforms and bunk assignments from the quartermaster. Get yourselves cleaned up and report for dinner in the dining hall at 1800 hours sharp." The Commander started to walk away then stopped and turned to the men standing beside their horses. "Those of you who have your own horse may claim a stall in the stable. You will be given army-issue tack. Dismissed!"

Jane's eyes popped open. Bunk assignments? Somehow, she hadn't thought that far. She had just assumed she would ride home every night. They were expecting her to stay overnight here? Jane's eyes shifted from side to side in a panic. What would she do? How would she be able to keep her secret if she was in a bunkhouse with a bunch of men? Her heart started pounding and she felt her knees start to buckle. She grabbed her stirrup to steady herself.

"You okay, John?"

Jane looked up to see Stephan Peters standing beside her.

"Y-y-yes. I guess I'm just a little dehydrated. Need some water," she stammered.

He pulled out a canteen. "Here. Have mine," he said as he offered it to her. "You're going to need to take care of yourself *and* your horse if you want to be a Sand Pounder."

"Thanks," she said, taking a drink of the metallic tasting water. "You're right. I'll do a better job tomorrow."

"Let me take your horse to the barn for you and get her all bedded down."

Jane smiled, warmed by his kindness. "I appreciate that, but I can do it," she said, handing him back his canteen.

"If you're sure . . ."

"I'm sure. Thanks." Jane watched him walk away and felt the same tingling sensation she had felt when she first met him. *Get over it, Jane,* she told herself. *He thinks you're a boy.*

Then her thoughts went back to the bunking predicament and the sense of panic returned. She forced herself to take long, deep breaths. Several seagulls flew overhead calling out to one another. She looked up at them, finding comfort in their familiarity.

As the sun slowly made its way west over the rolling ocean and a gentle breeze cooled the air, Jane led Star to her stall in the stables. She removed the heavy western saddle and replaced the bridle with a halter. She filled one bucket with grain, another with water, and the manger with hay. Once Jane had Star settled, she stepped out of the stall, swallowed, and lifted her chin as she unhooked Star's halter and hung it outside the stall. *I need to face this sometime,* she thought. *Here goes.*

She walked up the green concrete steps and entered the beautiful white building that served as the Coast Guard Headquarters. She appeared to be the last to arrive as it seemed all the recruits already carried a bundle of clothing. The Sand Pounders were issued uniforms provided by the Coast Guard. Jane stepped up to a long table, covered with tidy stacks of navy blue clothing, rows of boots and belts, and white caps.

The green-eyed woman Jane met earlier in the day was passing out the requisite items. She looked up from straightening a pile. "Well, you're one of the tiny ones. Let's see what I have here that will fit you." She quickly gathered several items and handed them to Jane. "I hope these will work," she said. Pointing to another table across the room she added, "Go over there to get your bunk assignment."

Jane thanked her and moved away from the table. She turned around and saw the table to which she had been directed. Several young men were standing in front of it, comparing sheets of paper and talking enthusiastically. Jane walked up to the table, squeezing between two men.

The Quartermaster looked up. "Name?"

"John Morris."

The Coast Guardsman flipped through several papers. Finding Jane's, he pulled it out of the stack and handed it to her.

"Thank you," Jane said meekly.

In a booming voice, the Quartermaster told the recruits they would be given their weapons once they passed their target shooting tests. They were then dismissed to find their quarters.

Jane dragged her feet over the short-clipped grass as she followed the men toward the buildings that housed the Coast Guardsmen's living quarters. Her head was lowered, her shoulders slumped. Her mind was filled with conflicting ideas, not the least of which was the notion of quitting all together. It just seemed that this idea was not going to work. Numb with fear, she followed the men through the green-painted wood doors. Once inside, she looked up. Ahead of her was not the long open room filled with bunk beds that she had envisioned. Instead, she was facing a narrow hallway lined with one door after another, some open, some closed. She glanced down at the paper with her assignment. "1-C" it read. Hers was the very first door. She pushed open the door and looked inside. Within the tiny room stood just one narrow bed, a chair, and hooks on the wall. A white towel hung from one of the hooks. But most important, there was just one bed! She couldn't believe it! She sagged against the doorframe. It didn't matter that the room was tiny, not even half the size of Star's stall. What mattered was that it was hers and hers alone. *Maybe this will work after all*, she thought.

She set her bundle on the bed and unfolded her uniform. The navy-blue top and bell-bottom pants were made of a light-weight wool. The shirt looked similar to the crackerjack uniforms worn by Navy sailors, with the squared-off collar hanging down the back. She was also given a white belt, white cap, and black boots.

The young woman reached over and shut the door. She took off her cowboy boots, jeans, hat, and button-down shirt, and replaced them with her new uniform. She was pleased that the wool was soft, not itchy as she expected. She looked around the room for a mirror. Finding none, she walked out of her room in search of the bathroom. She followed the sound of flushing toilets and splashing showers to the center of the barracks and came to an abrupt halt. Only one door was labeled "latrine." *Oh great,* she thought, *now what?* She remembered seeing bathrooms in the barn. She turned and hurried out the barrack's door.

Star nickered at her when she came out of the bathroom. "You recognized me? How do you like my new uniform?" Jane said, swaying from side to side as if showing off a new prom dress. Star tossed her head. Jane stepped into her horse's stall and started rubbing her down, humming as she went over her partner's well-muscled body and breathing in deeply of the sweet smell of horse.

"You coming to dinner?" a familiar voice called from a stall across the aisle.

Jane peeked over Star's stall door and saw the freckle-faced palomino rider grinning at her.

"Ah . . . sure," she said.

"Come on then," he said with a swing of his arm.

Jane latched Star's door and hurried to catch up.

"What's your name?" he asked.

"John Morris," she responded when she caught up. "Yours?"

"Timothy Tindall. You can call me Tim."

"You can call me John," Jane answered with a smile.

Tim looked at her and smirked. "With a baby face like yours, I think 'Pretty Boy' fits better."

As they walked to the mess hall, Tim asked, "Is that your horse?"

"Yes," Jane said, glancing back at the barn. "Your palomino is lovely."

"I wish he were mine. A rancher donated him to the Sand Pounders and said I could ride him until the war was over."

"So, he belongs to the army?" Jane asked.

"Yep."

11

August 1942

The driver of a long, green army stock trailer stopped for the night at the Portland International livestock barns. He unloaded and stabled his load of horses in the same stalls that had recently housed Japanese American families until internment camps were ready. The next morning, the driver called the post with his anticipated arrival time. Jane was notified by a Coast Guardsman to be at the barn at 10:00 a.m.

Right on time, the stock trailer pulled up to the barn. Jane had been waiting in front of the barn for not more than ten minutes, but long enough to chew her right thumbnail down to the nub. She dropped her hand to her side as the truck and trailer approached. She remained where she was standing until it came to a stop.

"Hey, young man," the truck driver said out his window. "I've got a load of horses for the Coast Guard. Do ya know who's takin' delivery?" he asked in a voice both flat and indifferent.

"I am, sir," Jane said, pleased that he had called her "young man."

"You goin' ta handle these horses yerself?"

"Yes, sir."

"Alright then. Let's get 'em unloaded," he said as he dropped down from the driver's seat in the cab and walked toward the rear of the trailer. He unlatched the gate and swung open the full-width door. The horses inside began snorting and stomping in anticipation of being released from their mobile prison.

Jane hurried to join the driver. She watched him enter the trailer and untie the end horse. "Step back, step back," the driver said. As the horse lowered his hind legs to the ground, Jane took the proffered lead rope and waited for the horse to lower his front legs. Once all four feet were out of the trailer the horse posed with his head and tail raised. He snorted and looked around.

Jane chuckled. "Easy boy. You're okay. You're going to like it here." She led the horse into the barn and put him in one of the stalls she had prepared earlier. By the time she returned, the driver, whose name she had neglected to ask, had already unloaded several horses and tied them to the paddock fence. As she approached, a loud banging came from within, and the trailer started rocking and shaking. A large bay gelding burst out of the back of the trailer, the lead rope flying out behind him. The frantic horse snorted and whinnied as it galloped past the line of horses tied to the fence, causing all the horses to paw and dance around a bit.

The gate to the paddock was open and he ran through. Jane hustled over and shut the gate, trapping the gelding inside. She stood at the gate and watched the horse gallop around the pen, his beautiful head up, his mane and tail flowing in the wind. A cloud of dust kicked up behind him. Occasionally, he stepped on his lead rope. The tug on his head caused him to stop, back up, then take off at a run again. Jane worried that the horse would get entangled in the rope and hurt himself. When the horse was on the far side of the pen, she opened the gate and entered, securing it behind her. She stood still and waited to see what the horse would do.

Seeing her, the gelding stopped and turned toward her, blowing out a loud breath of air through his flaring nostrils.

Jane took a few steps forward. "Hello, boy. Aren't you a pretty fellow," she said. The horse remained where he was. She stepped a few feet closer. "There you go. I'm not going to hurt you." Step by cautious step, Jane approached the horse. He kept his eyes on her but didn't move. His eyes showed fear but not meanness, so Jane reached up and unclipped the lead rope. The horse jerked away and started trotting around the pen. Jane went to the center of the pen and watched him. When the horse stopped and turned toward her, she stepped forward and to one side and motioned for him to go in the opposite direction. The horse responded by trotting off the other way. She repeated this exercise several times as the driver and more than a few of the Sand Pounders watched from outside the fence.

When the horse responded by merely walking, Jane said. "Whoa." The horse stopped and looked at her. She stepped up to him, clipped on the lead rope, and led him to the gate.

Tim was at the gate and opened it for her. "Guess you're not just a pretty boy after all," he said.

"Thanks, I guess," Jane said as she led the horse into the barn and settled him in a stall.

By the time Jane returned to the yard, the driver had finished unloading the remaining horses.

"Well, that's the last o' them," he said, handing her the lead rope to the one remaining horse. "I'll need you to sign the receipt." He turned and hustled back to the cab of his truck and returned with a clipboard. "Just sign here if ye would," he said, handing her a pen and pointing to the bottom of the paper.

Jane looked askance at the form, wondering if she was supposed to read it carefully.

"It just says I delivered fifteen Army horses from Fort Robinson to the Coast Guard station in Garibaldi and that they are all in good health."

Jane quickly counted the round rumps facing her and added three — yep, fifteen. The good health part remained to be seen. She shrugged her shoulders and signed the form.

"Thanks," he said, grabbing the clip board and climbing back behind the wheel of the truck. He slammed the door, started the engine, and pulled the long trailer out of the barnyard, the metal sides of the long rig shaking and rattling loudly.

Several new Sand Pounders approached. "Hey, John," said one.

Jane recognized Stephan's voice and turned to face him.

"I watched how you handled that big gelding. Impressive," he said. "Can I help you put the rest of them up?"

"I'd appreciate it, if you would," she said, avoiding his warm, kind eyes.

Stephan, Tim, and two other Sand Pounders approached the string of tied horses, talking softly, moving slowly, and using their hands to calm and comfort the new horses. They untied two at a time and led them into the barn, finding a stall for each. Once all the horses were in stalls, the young men took turns claiming the one they liked best. "This chestnut reminds me of my jumper," said Stephan.

"Doubt he could get over a one-foot log with those big feet," said another, giving Stephan a shove on his shoulder.

"How about this gray?" said another. "She has a kind eye."

"Oh, yeah, take her. You'll be an easy target for the Japs," joked a third man.

"I could put a dark blanket on her," said the first, still hanging over the stall door.

Stephan walked up to Jane. "I hear the Commander has assigned you to check out all the horses. He must be impressed with your horsemanship. After watching you, I can see why."

Jane bit her lip and nodded. She felt her cheeks get hot and she lowered her chin.

"I hope you don't find any rodeo broncs in the bunch. That big dark bay looked like he might be a handful—just the kind of horse that interests me."

"The Commander said they have all been bred and trained at the Army post in Nebraska," Jane said, looking down, smoothing her uniform, and adjusting her belt. "He just wants to know how well they have been prepared for what we will need them to do,"

"Why don't you come to the mess hall and have some lunch with us before you get started?" Stephan said.

"Sounds good," Jane said, still avoiding those beautiful eyes.

During the afternoon, Jane put one horse after another through its paces, first on the lunge line, then in the cross ties to groom and tack up, followed by a ride. Once mounted, she tested the "brakes" and the "steering" as she called halting and turning. She asked each horse to pick up the trot and turn circles in each direction, halt, back up, trot again. She picked up the canter on both leads and did some walk-to-canter transitions. This was followed by a cool-down walk with lots of neck-rubbing and soothing words.

As Jane worked each horse, several Sand Pounders watched from a distance. Their arms were folded across their chests and Jane could see they were talking to one another though she couldn't hear what they were saying. She hoped they were just scoping out future mounts for themselves and not critiquing her riding. She forced herself to look away and, like a barn-sour mare, return her concentration to the task at hand.

After she rode each horse, she wrote up a summary of her impressions. By the time the bell rang for dinner, Jane had ridden six of the fifteen horses. She knew tomorrow would be a busy day if she was to get all fifteen horses evaluated.

Star, whose head had hung over the stall door all day as though waiting for her turn, nickered when Jane returned to the stable leading the sixth horse. "Oh Star. I'm just doing a job. You don't need to worry. You're still my number one girl. Maybe I'll have time to ride you tomorrow."

By noon the next day, Jane had ridden four more horses. She sought out a table by herself in the mess hall with her lunch of a SPAM sandwich and an apple. As soon as she sat down, however, Tim Tindall scooted onto the bench beside her. "How is the riding going?" he said with a smile that melted some of his freckles together.

Jane swallowed her bite of sandwich before answering. "Good. The army has done a great job getting these horses rideable."

"Glad to hear it. Any favorites?"

"Yeah . . . Star."

Tim snorted. "You know what I mean."

Jane smiled. "I really like that little gray."

"She looks nice. Good gaits?"

"Very smooth trot and rolling canter. She's fun."

"So, does Star have some competition?" he said with a wink of his eye.

"Never," Jane said and took a bite of her apple.

"Have you ridden the dark bay gelding, yet?"

Jane shook her head. She didn't want to admit that she had purposely put off riding him, unsure of how it would go. But she knew she would have to face the music soon. *I'll work with him next,* she told herself.

As she ate her lunch, she thought about the immediate connection equestrians have with one another. When it came to horses, there was always something to talk about. She also realized that she was feeling more comfortable here; a camaraderie between the horsemen had developed in just three days at the post. She had only one complication yet to work out— all the showers were in the latrine. So far, she had just avoided taking a shower. But that could not go on much longer, especially if the gelding put her in the dirt.

12

August 1942

Jane walked down the center aisle of the barn to stall number thirteen, the stall that housed the big, dark-bay gelding. Sweat was trickling irritatingly down her back. *I hope his stall number isn't a bad omen*, she thought. The horse was calmly munching on his hay but lifted his head when she opened the stall door. "Hi, fella," she said, forcing herself to breathe slowly. The horse snorted and moved away. "Let's get to know each other better, whaddya say?" She moved toward him, one hand outstretched, the other clasping the halter with the lead rope attached.

The horse changed direction and moved the other way, but Jane was relieved to see he didn't turn his hind end toward her.

Focusing on his shoulder, Jane moved toward him again. This time, he stayed where he was but watched her with a look of suspicion, his head cocked to one side, the whites of his eyes visible.

"It's okay. I'm not going to hurt you," she cooed as she placed the lead rope over his muscular neck and slipped the halter over his head. Taking hold of the lead rope, she turned and started to walk out of the stall. As soon as the slack in the rope disappeared, Jane felt a sharp tug. She turned to see the gelding's head up, and his front legs braced. Knowing she couldn't win a tug-o-war with a thousand-pound animal, she unhooked the lead rope from the ring on the halter, left the stall, and selected a long crop from the tack room wall where several were neatly hung.

When she returned to the stall, the gelding had resumed eating his hay. This time, when she entered the stall, the horse did not move away, but still watched her with wide eyes as she approached his head. Jane clipped the lead rope to his halter again, then retrieved the crop from where she had tucked it in the back of her belt. She used the end of the crop to rub his neck and shoulder as she hummed a calming song.

Feeling the horse relax, she turned toward the stall door. "Walk," she said as she placed one foot forward. The horse didn't move.

"Walk," she said again, this time tapping the horse's side lightly with the tasseled end of the crop. The gelding jerked his head up and started moving forward. Jane stayed by his head and kept walking. The horse stayed beside her. "Good boy," she crooned. "Good boy."

"Impressive."

Startled, Jane squinted and looked into the darkness of the barn's aisle. Standing across from the gelding's stall was Stephan. He stepped up to her. "You handled that really well," he said. "What is your plan now?"

Looking at the gelding, more to hide her blushing cheeks than anything else, she said, "I'm going to tack him up then lunge him," she said. Jane knew that a horseman such as Stephan would know that lunging a horse on a long line, having him walk, trot and canter in a circle around her, was a good way of assessing both his movements and his temperament. She clipped the horse in the cross ties and headed to the tack room to gather a saddle and bridle.

Following right behind, Stephan said, "Are you going to use one of the army-issue McClellan saddles that just arrived?"

Jane scrunched her nose at the thought. She wasn't very impressed with the quality of the saddles the army had sent. She was used to her fine English saddle and her sturdy western one. "I think I'll use my western saddle. I noticed the army saddles don't have a horn and, well . . . with this guy, I might need something to hang on to."

Stephan chuckled. "You're right there, that's for sure. Mind if I hang around and watch? I have a couple of hours before my assigned target shooting practice time."

"Sure," Jane said, though not sure how she really felt about it. Stephan was an accomplished show jumper. She felt the pressure building inside her to look good. *What if he thinks I'm a terrible rider?* she thought. Trying her best to exhibit an air of confidence, Jane grabbed a long canvas rope for lunging, and her saddle and bridle.

Stephan helped her groom the gelding and placed the heavy western saddle gently on his back. Both Jane and Stephan stepped back to see how the horse would respond. Pleased that he just stood quietly, Jane put the bit in the gelding's mouth and slipped the headstall over his ears. Stephen tightened the cinch slowly.

Jane grabbed the lunge line, hooked it to the ring on the bit, and led the horse to the paddock. Standing in the center, she shooed the horse away. The gelding immediately snorted and trotted off, his head high in the air. He trotted to the end of the long lunge line and started moving in a large circle. Jane let him trot several revolutions before turning him in and changing direction. With a squeal and a buck, he took off in a canter.

"Easy boy, just trot," she said, giving a slight tug on the lunge line. The horse shook his head in complaint but slowed to a trot.

"He looks fine," Stephan said from where he stood with his arms folded over the top rail of the fence. "Would you feel okay if I rode him?"

"You want to?"

"Yes. He's a big boy, a perfect horse for me," Stephan said. "I think I'd like him to be my mount for the beach patrol."

"But yesterday you talked about the chestnut," Jane said quizzically.

"I like the chestnut, too. But this big bay has me interested," Stephan said.

Jane pulled on the lunge line and brought the horse to her. She stood in front of him, watching his reaction as Stephan adjusted the stirrups. The gelding rolled his eyes a few times but otherwise didn't complain. Jane unclipped the lunge line. Stephan clasped the reins and calmly placed a boot in the left stirrup. "Here goes," he said, giving Jane a wink. Putting his weight in the stirrup, he smoothly pushed up and swung his right leg over the back of the saddle. He gently sat down in the saddle. The gelding stood stiff legged, his ears pinned back.

Stephan stroked the horse's neck. "There's a good boy," he said, his voice kind and gentle. After a few minutes of sitting quietly, Stephan said, "Let's go for a walk." He tapped the gelding's barrel with his long legs. The horse lifted his head and bolted forward, sending Stephan head over teakettle off the back to land with a *humph* in the soft dirt.

Pushing down her natural response to express concern, Jane tried to respond as she felt a man would. "Whoa, cowboy! Is that how you were taught to ride?" Jane said as she ran over to him.

Stephan pushed himself up to his knees. "Sure wasn't expecting that," he said as he brushed off his shirt.

"But are you okay?" Jane asked, dropping her voice an octave.

Stephan scrambled to his feet and brushed off his pants. "Yeah. Just surprised me."

Jane and Stephan turned and looked at the gelding. The large horse stood across the paddock staring back at them, breathing heavily.

"Now that we know we can't trust him, let me give him a try," Jane said.

"Be my guest," Stephan said.

Jane walked up to the gelding and took his reins. Jane was aware that her manner of cooing and coddling a horse was not considered very manly. But she did not know any other way to work with horses. She lowered her voice so as not to be heard as she addressed the gelding. "Well, that wasn't very nice, old boy. I expect much better behavior out of you." Feeling the butterflies dancing in her stomach, she rubbed his neck and combed her fingers through his long mane as she moved toward the saddle. She pulled on the stirrup, making the saddle roll back and forth. The horse remained calm. She shortened the stirrups on both sides. "See, I'm not going to hurt you," she whispered. The gelding turned his head and watched her as she moved from side to side.

"Okay, buddy. Let's try this again, shall we?" she said, trying to keep her nervous energy suppressed. Facing the saddle, Jane grasped the left stirrup and took in three deep breaths through her nose, letting each one out through her mouth. She gracefully mounted the horse and sat in the saddle. The horse's ears pinned back but he didn't move. Jane rubbed his neck on both sides, whispering compliments to the horse, then picked up the reins. She turned his head, first one way, then the other, and back again several times. Taking a deep breath and letting it out slowly, she made a kissing sound followed by a cluck and said, "Walk."

The horse moved forward without hesitation.

For the next twenty minutes, Jane asked the horse to walk, then halt, then walk again. She asked him to circle in both directions, halt, and back up. Finally, she kissed, clucked, and said, "Trot." The horse picked up a swinging trot.

Jane brought him to a halt in front of Stephan. She bounced off the horse and handed the reins to Stephan. "Try him again," she said with a smile.

Stephan, not as sure of himself as before, hesitated. He took a deep breath and let it out with a puff. "Okay. Here goes."

Five hours later, Jane reported to the Commander's office in the beautiful, white headquarters building. Handing him the report on each horse she added, "I don't want to be presumptuous and tell you what to do, but . . ." She paused.

"Please go on," the Commander said.

"Well, I would like to recommend that you assign the big, bay gelding to Stephan Peters."

Talk at the dinner table was all about Stephan getting dumped by the big gelding.

"So, word around the post is that the famous show jumper got dumped today," said one recruit as he sat down across from Stephan.

"The little horsey get the better of you?" taunted the wise guy sitting next to him as he poked him in the ribs with his elbow. The men around the table guffawed.

Stephan looked down at his plate and twisted his fork in his mashed potatoes.

"Hey, buddy. Don't take it too hard. We've all been there, haven't we, guys?" said an older, more compassionate man.

Each of the men at the table started sharing the stories of their worst falls. The stories got louder and more boisterous with each telling.

Jane kept quiet as she listened to the unrelenting teasing. No mention was made of how successful Stephan's second attempt had been, so she decided to chime in. "You should have seen Stephan ride that big boy his second try. He had him eating out of his hand," she said.

Stephan looked over at her and smiled, showing how happy he was to be rescued. "I wouldn't go that far, but at least I stayed in the saddle. 'Course that was after you got him all tuned up like an Indianapolis race car."

13

August 1942

Jane lay in her bed, watching the clock with its fluorescent hands rotate ever so slowly in the darkness. She listened, waiting for the sounds coming from the latrine and hall to cease and the last of the room doors to slam shut. Then she waited some more. Her muscles were sore from two solid days of riding. The horse smell was clinging to her skin and short hair. She desperately needed a shower. In the days she had been at the post, she hadn't once been brave enough to risk entering the latrine, let alone take a shower. She made up her mind that tonight would be the night.

The greenish yellow lines of the clock's hands, made fluorescent with radium, moved gradually around the clock face until they pointed straight up — twelve o-clock. She threw back her blanket and stepped to the door. Pressing her ear against the cool wood, she listened. All she could hear was the gentle patting of raindrops against the blacked-out windowpane across the tiny room. She grabbed the towel from the hook on the wall and silently turned the knob. The door squeaked on its hinges, causing her to stop moving it. Now she could hear snoring coming from behind several closed doors. Taking a deep breath, she opened the door wider and slipped into the hallway. Tiptoeing down the unlit hall, she made her way to the latrine by running her hand down the walls and counting the doors. She knew the door to the latrine was the seventh door on the left. Placing her hand on the swinging door, she looked quickly over each shoulder into the darkness then pushed her way in.

A single bulb hung from the center of the room, dimly lighting the unadorned room. Small, gray ceramic tiles covered the floor and halfway up the walls. On her left was a row of urinals. Straight ahead were a half dozen wooden doors providing privacy for the toilets. Across from the wall of urinals was a row of shower stalls that were covered with curtains. She wanted to jump for joy as her fears of a common shower were relieved. She hurried into the first stall, pulled off her clothing and turned on the water.

The hot water felt both relaxing and rejuvenating on her sore muscles. It made her want to sing for joy . . . but she dared not. Just as she started massaging the shampoo into her scalp, she heard a voice. She froze.

"Hey, who's in here showering at this hour?"

The shampoo ran down her face and stung her eyes. Her heart pounded so loudly she was sure the intruder could hear it. Jane swallowed and said with her low voice, "It's John," she said, gathering the shower curtain around her and peeking around. Standing in front of the urinal was Tim. Jane jerked her head back behind the curtain.

"Oh, John, what are you doing up so late?" Tim said over his shoulder.

Jane reached over and turned off the water. "I didn't have time to take a shower earlier," she said as she reached around the curtain, groping for her towel.

"Here you go," Tim said, shoving the towel in her hand.

"Uh . . . thanks," she said, her teeth chattering with nerves not cold. *I hope he doesn't stay long*, she thought as she wrapped the towel around her body.

"So, how did the riding of the new horses go today? Did you find any good ones?"

Oh great. What a time to visit. "Yeah. Sure." Jane stayed huddled in the corner of the shower stall.

"What about the big bay? I heard that fancy show jumper, Stephan, had a hard time with him."

Is he ever going to leave? "He got it worked out," she said, trying her best to put an end to the conversation.

"You ever coming out?"

"Uh . . . in a minute. You go ahead and go back to bed," Jane said.

"Well, okay. I guess I'll see you in the morning." Jane heard his footsteps slap the tile floor of the latrine, then stop. "You better not stay up too late yourself," he said, before pushing the door open.

Jane waited a few minutes before peeking around the curtain. She did not see any sign of Tim or anyone else. With the towel wrapped tightly around her, and her heart still pounding wildly, she grabbed her government-issue boxer shorts and crewneck T-shirt that she was using for pajamas. Safely concealed behind the shower curtain, she got dressed and hurried back to her room, her wet hair sending droplets rolling down her back.

14

August 1942

A hot breakfast of bacon and eggs in the mess hall was interrupted when the Commander entered the room. Immediately, all chatter stopped, replaced by the sound of scraping chairs as the men stood.

"At ease, men," said the Commander. "I have here, your mount assignments." He waved a sheet of paper over his head for all to see. "Those of you who did not come with your own horse have been assigned one provided by the Army, along with a saddle and bridle. Your first job today, and every day hereafter, will be to care for your horse. You are to make sure that your horse, and his stall and tack, are always spotless. That your horse is well-fed and kept sound." He held up the sheet of paper again. "I will be posting the assignments by stall number in the barn. Enjoy your breakfast but be mounted and in formation on the parade field at 1000 hours. Resume eating." The Commander turned and left the hall.

Jane looked around. Excitement filled the air as the men started talking about their new mounts. She looked over at Stephan who was sitting across from her. "Do you think you'll get the bay?"

He shoved a spoonful of eggs into his mouth and mumbled, "I hope so."

Jane suddenly lost her appetite in her eager desire to get to the barn to see the assignments. She knew each of the horses now and felt a bit of ownership. She wanted the best for them. She also hoped the Commander had taken her recommendation to assign the bay to Stephan.

By the time she reached the barn, there was already a group of men around the list. As soon as a man found his mount, he left the group to walk down the aisle and meet his new partner. Jane stepped up to the list. She ran her finger down the numbers to thirteen, the big bay. Across from that number was the name, "Stephan Peters." Jane smiled. As she turned away from the bulletin board, she bumped right into Stephan as he peered over her. "Did you make that happen?" he asked.

"I just made a recommendation," Jane said, feeling her cheeks get hot again.

"Well, let me say thanks. I promise I won't let him throw me again."

At 1000 hours sharp, the Commander marched across the parade field in front of a long line of sharply dressed riders sitting atop freshly groomed mounts. Several horses tossed their heads, a few pawed the ground, cutting into the grass that had been soaked by the previous night's rain. But the men sat straight and still. Only their eyes moved as they followed the approaching Commander.

"Gentlemen, we will begin today's drill by reciting the Coast Guard Ethos."

Without hesitation, all the Sand Pounders boldly recited the Ethos they had all memorized. Jane felt her heart swell with pride again as she barked out the words.

I am a Coast Guardsman.
I serve the people of the United States.
I will protect them.
I will defend them.
I will save them.
I am their shield.
For them I am Semper Paratus.
I live the Coast Guard core values.
I am proud to be a Coast Guardsman.
We are the United States Coast Guard.

The Commander paced back and forth in front of the line of horses. He stopped and turned to face his recruits. "With the exception of the few horses who are privately owned," the Commander nodded at Jane and a few other men, "the horses you sit astride at this time have come to us from the Army. The U.S. Army has purchased over twenty-six thousand horses since 1941. More than three thousand of these horses have been assigned to the Coast Guard for our new mounted patrol along both coasts. The tack has been provided by the Army Remount Service, but your uniforms have been proudly provided by the U.S. Coast Guard."

Jane kept her eyes glued to the Commander, but she dropped her little fingers to tickle Star's withers as she listened.

"We will now begin our mounted training," the Commander said. As soon as the Commander said those words, an explosive device went off across the field, piercing the air with an enormous boom. Most of the horses jumped or spooked. Tim's palomino spun, sending the freckle-faced boy to the ground. Jumping up, he grabbed the reins before his horse could bolt away. He worked at calming his horse by stroking his neck. His previously clean uniform now had a large dark spot on his right hip where he had landed on the wet grass. Star did nothing more than jerk her head up and prick her ears in the direction of the blast. Jane glanced down the row of dancing horses to find Stephan. Relieved that he was still on his horse, she was pleased to see that he had the horse calmed down already.

A few minutes later, a second blast went off and there was more snorting and prancing by several of the horses, but the men managed to keep them under control. Tim remounted, none the worse for wear with only his pride damaged.

"As you can see, men," the Commander shouted. "We need to be prepared for anything, including bombs and rifle fire. So, let's get to work!"

For the next two weeks, the men drilled their horses with long hours on the parade grounds and along the sandy shores of Tillamook Bay. Jane couldn't have been happier spending all those hours in the saddle, walking, trotting, cantering, making quick turns on the hindquarters. She loved cantering through the waves as they slapped the shore, feeling the salty breeze across her face. She swallowed a giggle with each joyous stride. It was easy to forget that this was to prepare for war. . . until they were assigned their weapons.

The Commander had watched the daily progress of both the horses and their riders as they went through their drills. At last, he felt the time was right to up the ante. Each rider was assigned a rifle, binoculars, and a thirty-five-pound radio.

Standing in front of his newly equipped corps of Sand Pounders, the Commander shouted orders. "Your job is to patrol the beaches and be on the lookout for any evidence of enemy activity. You are to immediately report anything you find that is suspicious. It is not your job to engage in battle unless necessary. That is the Army's and Navy's job."

Jane listened as the Commander repeated these instructions over and over. Still, she felt her body tense and she clenched her teeth. The riding she could do. She was even competent on the shooting range. But could she ever shoot a real person? Was that what her brother was doing in the Navy?

15

August 1942

One night in mid-August, Jane received a letter. It came in an envelope addressed to "John Morris" from her best friend, Jeannie. She hurried to the privacy of her room in the barracks, eager to read what Jeannie had written. She plopped on her bed and ripped open the envelope. Inside, she was surprised to find two letters. One was from Thomas Kato and the other from her brother. She felt tears sting behind her eyes and her throat constrict as she smoothed out the rumpled papers. She pursed her lips, took a deep breath, and started reading her brother's letter. The first thing she noticed was the date: June 23, 1942. It had taken two months for the letter to reach her.

June 23, 1942

Dear Jane,

I know it has been a long time since I have written a letter to you. It has been hard to find time to write and harder still to find opportunities to mail a letter once it is written. Please always remember that I am holding your hand in mine as I fight to keep you and our country safe.

Jane paused. *Maybe he really is shooting people,* she thought. She continued reading, trying her best to decipher his messy scribbles and what might have been censored.

I am proud to report that from June 4th to June 7th, I was involved in a great and successful battle in the Pacific. Our cryptographers, that means codebreakers, discovered a plan by the Japanese ▮▮▮▮▮▮▮▮▮▮ ▮▮▮▮▮▮ ▮▮▮▮▮▮▮▮▮▮, which are the islands halfway between North America and Asia. Unlike Pearl Harbor, this time, we were ready for them. We took out four of their aircraft carriers that had attacked Pearl Harbor. Sadly, we lost the carrier Yorktown and the destroyer Hammann, and 307 brave Americans. But after the battle ended, we had decisively defeated the Japanese in their attempt to control the Pacific.

I must tell you that I write this after the battle was over. During the battle, I was scared that I would never return home. There is nothing good about war, and I hope our success at defeating the enemy in this battle will help it end soon. I am fighting to keep you safe. Read the Bible I gave you and pray for me. I miss home very much. I often think about you and imagine you riding Star along the beach with the wind blowing through your long hair. I hope you are keeping a good eye on Grandma and Aunt Molly. Please help them all you can.

Your brother, Luke

Jane felt a tear trickle down her cheek as she read Luke's letter for the second time. Had she made the right decision to join the Sand Pounders? Would Luke be proud of her or angry with her? He was fighting to keep her safe, yet here she was, putting herself in grave danger. She stood up and paced her room, marched to the blacked-out window, and back to the door and pulled it open. She hurried out the barracks and ran to the barn.

Star was nestled down in the straw bedding of her stall. The mare lifted her head when Jane entered the stall but didn't stand. Jane kneeled next to Star's head and threw her arms around the horse's neck. She buried her face in Star's mane and breathed in deeply the sweet perfume of horse. "Oh Star. Are we doing the right thing?" she whispered. Star kept her muzzle resting in the straw.

When Jane got control of her emotions, she returned to the barracks. She sat back on her bed and pulled the second letter out of the envelope. It was from Thomas.

August 1, 1942

Dear Jane,

I hope this letter finds you well. How are things in Tillamook? It is almost time for school to start again. That is hard to believe. So much has happened to me that Tillamook High School seems nothing more than a dream.

Speaking of school, we have a school of sorts here. It is held in the barracks. We don't have any textbooks, so the teachers have no choice but to simply lecture all day. Several of the teachers are bused across the California border from Oregon. Most are from Klamath Falls and a small town close by called Malin. Some of the teachers are okay, most are not very good. None of them stay long. I don't think they knew what they were getting into when they signed up! Most are fresh out of college and probably expected there would be desks and books and things like that. Can't blame them for quitting...I would, too.

My one pleasure is playing baseball on the sandy field behind the barracks. We boys formed several teams and set up a tournament. It helps us get through these horribly hot days and gives us something to look forward to.

I have thought many times about running away but I don't want to hurt my father.

I hope you are doing well and staying safe. How is our kitty doing?

Sincerely, Your Friend,

Thomas

Jane hadn't given the Katos' kitty a second thought since dropping it off at Jeannie's barn. Jeannie had promised she would look after it. Jane hoped that someday she would be able to return it to the Katos. *Will this nightmare ever end?* she wondered.

16

September 1942

Jane stepped out of the barracks before anyone else was even stirring. She stopped and looked to the pink sunrise. It was the first day of September, the best month of the year in her estimation. The coastal air had a crispness about it that made her feel alive, and the sun liked to make its presence known more often than usual for Oregon. She breathed deeply, letting the air out through her mouth in a huff. She smiled and turned toward the stables.

"Good morning, Star," she said as she entered the barn. Several horses greeted her with nickers but Star's deep, marish rumbling was all she heard as she walked down the barn aisle. She stopped in front of Star's stall. "Today is a big day, girl. Today we will get our assignment. We are actually going to be Sand Pounders for real!" Excitement, accompanied by a tinge of nervousness, sent a shiver down her spine.

Jane rubbed the star on the mare's face before turning and entering the feed room to get her some hay and grain. As the horse munched contentedly on the hay, Jane grabbed the manure fork and wheelbarrow and started cleaning the stall. As she worked, her mind was buzzing with questions. Where would she be sent? Who would be her partner? And most of all: Was she really up to the task? She leaned the fork against the wall of the stall and approached her horse. Star lifted her head, her warm, brown eyes peering into Jane's soul. Jane held Star's muzzle in her hands and kissed the soft skin between the nostrils.

"Are you some kind of girl?"

Jane jumped. Star pulled back her head and snorted. Jane felt her cheeks flush. She looked over her shoulder. Hanging over the stall door was Tim.

"What?" Jane said in her man voice.

"I thought only girls kissed their horses," he said with a chuckle.

"Oh . . . ah," Jane stammered, searching for an appropriate response. Coming up with nothing, she just shrugged her shoulders, grabbed the manure fork, and returned to mucking the stall.

By the time Jane finished cleaning Star's stall, the other Sand Pounders had arrived in the barn and were just getting started on their chores. Jane returned to the barracks and dressed in her Coast Guard uniform then went to the mess hall for breakfast. She had little appetite. Her stomach seemed to be twisted in anxious knots. She forced herself to eat a piece of toast and drink a glass of milk.

Once breakfast was finished, the bell clanged, calling the Sand Pounders to the parade grounds. The Commander was waiting as they arrived. The men lined up and stood at attention.

"At ease, men," the Commander said. Jane dropped her chin and shoulders, but her body refused to relax.

"Today you will receive your orders for your first beach patrol assignment. Each team will consist of two riders. You will be given a two-mile stretch of beach to cover. You are to work in pairs so that one man can hold down a suspect while the other goes to get help by using the nearest of the special telephone boxes that have been placed along the beaches at about quarter-mile lengths. If no boxes are available, you will use your radios. Most of our areas will require round-the-clock patrols. Two pairs will be assigned to those areas so that two men will be on duty while two men will be off."

The Commander unbuttoned his jacket and took it off, revealing a crisp white shirt, dampened by sweat. For the first time, Jane noticed how hot it was for a fall day in Oregon. She raised her arm and wiped her brow with her sleeve.

"Now, to continue," the Commander said. "We have secured housing for each team. Don't expect the Ritz." A chuckle rolled through the row of men. "Some of you will have to begin your assignment by building corrals for the horses. You will also need to secure hay and grain from the nearest source. Does anyone have any questions?"

Tim raised his hand.

"Yes, Coast Guardsman Tindal?"

"Sir, when will we be given our assignments?"

"They are, even now, being posted in the headquarters building. Dismissed."

In a blur of navy blue uniforms, the Sand Pounders turned on their heels and ran to the front door of the white headquarters building. Their boots made loud banging sounds on the wooden stairs and porch as they hurried in the green front doors.

The woman behind the desk jerked her head up, her bespectacled eyes wide, surprised by the sudden, loud interruption of her quiet morning. Without saying a word, she pointed toward the side wall.

Jane squeezed her way between two taller men dominating the front row. Quickly scanning down the list, she found her name. Her partner: Stephan Peters. Her assignment: Lincoln City. She turned around, once again nearly bumping into Stephan.

"Howdy Pawdner," he said with a tip of his sailor cap and a grin on his face.

"I'll be glad to work with you," Jane said, avoiding eye contact.

"Same here. Let's get ready to go."

By the time lunch was over in the mess hall, several trucks and trailers were lined up by the barn. Stacks of tack, horse gear, and duffle bags holding the Sand Pounders' belongings were strewn across the gravel drive.

Jane and Stephan were joined by Tim and his partner, a man Jane didn't know but had seen while training. Jane stuck out her hand.

"Hi, I'm John Morris."

"Chip Armstrong."

"Oh, Chip, you're a rodeo rider, aren't you? I recognize the name," Jane said while shaking his calloused hand.

"Yep, until the Pendleton Roundup got put on hold due to the war. Now I'm trying to help get this war over by being a Sand Pounder. Say, you have awfully soft hands there, cowboy," Chip said.

Jane pulled her hand away.

"John, it's our turn to load up," Stephan called from across the stable yard.

Jane grabbed her gear and put it in the back of the pickup hooked to the eight-horse stock trailer that would carry two teams of four south on Highway 101.

"John," Stephan called out. "Can you put Star in first? It might make Big Bay happier."

"Is that what you're calling him?" she asked Stephan as she led Star from the barn.

"What?"

"Big Bay. Is that what you're calling him?"

"Seems like the perfect name to me," Stephan said with a shrug.

After loading their horses, Jane, Stephan, Tim, Chip and four other Sand Pounders she hadn't met before squeezed into a truck. For an hour, they followed the trailer south on 101. Finally, the Coast Guardsman who was towing the horse trailer pulled off the highway and headed west toward Neskowin Beach. The uncomfortable truck carrying the men bounced around the corner in pursuit. Stopping in the tiny town of Neskowin, the Sand Pounders tumbled out of the back of the truck. The four who were assigned to this beach gathered their equipment and tack and unloaded their horses. Jane climbed back in the truck and looked out the back as they pulled away. The men left behind were holding lead ropes attached to horses and looking around. She guessed they were a bit bewildered, as she was sure she would be at the next stop.

A few miles farther down the road, they approached the northern edge of Lincoln City. Instead of turning toward the beach at Lincoln City, the driver turned toward a collection of tiny homes situated on the shores of Devils Lake. The three-mile-long lake flowed to the ocean through D River, claimed to be the shortest river in the world. The horse trailer came to a stop in front of one of the tiny houses. The driver got out and walked up to the troop transporter. "This is home sweet home for the four of you," he said. "Get your gear and horses. I've more deliveries to make."

17

September 1942

Jane and her three teammates led their horses to the lake behind the house to get a drink before tying their mounts to some of the gnarled, wind-swept evergreens that tilted toward the east. Jane grabbed her gear and, with a pounding heart, headed for the tiny house to check out the living arrangements.

She set her duffel bag on the porch and opened the sagging screen door. It squeaked on rusted hinges as she pulled it open. The wooden front door, with its peeling blue paint, was unlocked and it opened easily. Picking up her bag, she stepped inside.

Jane dropped her duffel bag with a plop and lowered her gun from off her shoulder. She looked around. Surrounding her were the remains of someone's home, or perhaps a city person's beach retreat; she wasn't sure. How the Coast Guard acquired it, she didn't know. But here she stood in this tiny house that she was supposed to share with three men, all near her age or slightly older. *What have I done?* she asked herself. Then her thoughts went to her brother and what he must be going through to protect the country. *I can do this,* she scolded herself.

She continued surveying the house. The room in which she stood was the living room, furnished with a lumpy couch at one end and a small metal-framed and Formica-topped table with four chairs at the other. An ash-filled fireplace promised a source of heat for the upcoming winter. Through an open doorway, Jane caught a glimpse of what must be the kitchen. A closed door suggested the presence of a bathroom or bedroom.

Loud footsteps echoed behind her and she turned to see Stephan enter the little front room.

"Hey, this is pretty nice."

Jane rolled her eyes.

"No, really. I've heard stories of Sand Pounders on the East Coast—North Carolina—living in old slave quarters." Stephan pushed past her, avoiding tripping on her bag, and walked across the room. "Let's see what's in here," he said as he opened the door. "Ah . . . the bedroom. And look at this, indoor plumbing," he shouted from inside the darkened room.

He soon reappeared, a grin on his face. "Yep, we struck it rich with this one. Come on in and claim your bunk."

Jane sighed, resigning herself to her fate. Her secret would be hard to keep now. She bent down and picked up her bag and walked into the room. With clenched jaw, she threw her bag on the lower bed of one of the two bunks

The rest of the unusually hot September day was spent building a corral for the four horses and dividing up chores and patrol duties. Jane mounted Star and left to find a source of food for the horses while Stephan left on Big Bay to find food for the humans. Tim and Chip took the trail along D River to start the first patrol.

Jane rode north along the narrow, unpaved road that provided access to the cabins surrounding the lake. After passing a few houses, Jane came across an older man standing at his mailbox. He looked up, startled to see a horseman approaching.

"Good Evening," Jane said in her manliest voice.

The man smiled and nodded.

"I'm one of the Sand Pounders."

"Sand Pounders?" he responded while scratching the stubble on his chin.

"We are a unit of the Coast Guard assigned to patrol the beach here at Lincoln City. It will be our job to keep our shores safe from the enemy."

"Ah. The wife will be happy to hear that. She's been afraid to leave the house. I'm Dr. Dennis Dirksen, but everyone around here just calls me Doc."

"Nice to meet you, Doc. Perhaps you can help me. We have just arrived and are in need of feed for our horses. Might you know where we can acquire some hay and grain?"

"Sure do. I have a friend up in Otis Junction who can fix you right up. I'll give him a call. Where you stayin'?"

Jane pointed back down the road. "The first house. The white one with the blue door."

"Oh. The Itami place." He looked down and shook his head. "Too bad about them."

"What's the matter?" Jane asked.

"Nice Japanese family owned that house. Mr. Itami ran a grocery store over in the valley. McMinnville, I think. They loved to come here and stay in their cabin. Fish . . . play on the beach . . . fly kites . . . just like any family. The wife and I had them over for dinner a few times. I'm a retired doctor so they called on me to treat the kids on occasion. I liked those kids. Then they got shipped off to an internment camp somewhere. I don't know where." His mouth melted into a frown.

Jane's thoughts went to the Katos and she felt her heart ache.

"Well, I guess that's neither here nor there," Doc said, shrugging his shoulders. "I'll get ahold of my friend. He has a truck. He'll get you all set by the morning. Surely you've got enough grass to last you that long. Nobody has mowed for quite a while."

Jane smiled. "I sure appreciate it. Thanks." She turned Star back and trotted down the road in the darkening evening. A full moon replaced the setting sun. Her thoughts dwelled on the Katos, and she wondered if the full moon was lighting their way, too.

Back at the house, Jane took advantage of the absence of the others to take a quick shower and change into night clothes in the tiny bathroom. She hung her uniform in the miniature closet and set about polishing her boots while she waited for Stephan to return. Her stomach growled in complaint from not being introduced to food since lunch, several hours earlier.

The night was illuminated only by the moon as Stephan returned to the house with a bag of canned goods from the grocery store in Lincoln City. "I didn't know what you liked so I just bought what I liked," he said as he dropped the bag on the chipped Formica of the kitchen counter.

"At this point, anything will do," said Jane as she sorted through the cans. "I found a neighbor who is helping us get feed."

"Oh, good," Stephan said as he rifled through the drawers in search of a can opener. "You ready to start our first day of patrol tomorrow?"

"Yes. I'm eager to get going. That's what I signed up for."

"Me, too," Stephan said as he poured a can of beans into a pan and turned on the electric burner.

Morning came far earlier than expected. Chip and Tim stomped into the house, dropping their thirty-five-pound radio on the floor with a thud that shook the house and awakened Jane and Stephan. Jane got up and hurried into the tiny bathroom to dress. Coming out, she blushed to see the tired men in nothing more than their underwear, getting into bed. She quickly turned her back. "How did it go?" she asked over her shoulder.

"Nothing but a few locals on the beach last night," mumbled Chip as he crawled under his covers. As soon as his head hit the pillow, Jane heard the deep, rhythmic breathing of slumber.

Jane and Stephan speedily tacked up their horses and set out for the beach in Lincoln City. To get to the beach, they rode along a footpath that followed the edge of D River. When they reached the grass-covered sand dunes that bordered the shore, Jane stopped. She breathed in the cool morning air, feeling the wind brush past her cheeks. The clear sky was a welcome sight as the sun climbed over the coastal mountains behind her. The waves crashed against the shore, nearly drowning out the sound of the gulls calling to one another as they searched for their morning meal of fish. The beauty of the windswept dunes and curling waves rolling along the shore filled her with awe. This was her home. This was where she belonged — on the back of a horse overlooking the vast ocean. She smiled.

"What's that grin on your face for?"

She turned toward Stephan. "Oh, nothing. I just love the beach and the ocean."

"Yep. It's mighty pretty. But we aren't here to enjoy the scenery. We have a job to do. I'll head out first. You follow me in a few minutes."

Jane watched Stephan trot off and splash across the shallow river as it flowed into the gray waters of the Pacific Ocean. Star tossed her head, eager to be off as well.

"Easy, girl," Jane said as she stroked her neck. "We'll be going soon." She pulled out her binoculars and scanned the horizon in both directions. No one was on the beach nor out on the water, not even a local fishing boat. She put her binoculars back in her saddle bag. Figuring that Stephan was the required distance ahead, she tapped her calves against Star's sides. "Let's go, girl," she said.

For the next twelve hours, Jane and Stephan rode up and down the beach at Lincoln City, covering the area to both the north and south of D River. They often stopped and visited with the locals who were excited to see them. Jane couldn't help but notice the high school girls giggling and flirting with Stephan. Stephan's handsome face and friendly demeanor made him an immediate favorite. Jane felt a twinge of jealousy twist her insides. She bit the inside of her cheek. *This is silly,* she told herself. She shook her head and shrugged her shoulders to dislodge the feeling. She dug her heels in Star's side, sending the mare off at a canter.

18

October 1942

For the first month, all went smoothly. The weather was pleasant, though getting progressively cooler. The locals began looking for them as they rode past, waving and calling out their names. The friendly people rewarded their presence with gifts of food for the Coast Guardsmen and treats for the horses. To Jane, it seemed this job, though important, was going to be much easier than she expected.

Jane enjoyed visiting with Dr. Dirksen, down the lane. She met his wife and learned their names were Dennis and Melanie, long-time Lincoln City residents. Melanie loved baking when she could secure enough sugar, and often sent her husband to bring them warm goodies.

The second month, the two teams traded shifts. Jane and Stephan took the night shift. Riding out at sunset on the second night, Jane noticed a bank of clouds far off on the horizon. She didn't think much of it at the time. But, as she rode along the damp sand, the wind picked up. Black clouds rolled in from the west as the waves grew wild. A flash of lightning stabbed the ocean. The accompanying thunderclap rocked the beach, angry and alarming. Star snorted and tossed her head. Jane took a shuddering breath.

Jane and Stephan completed their first patrol of the south side of the river and headed north, Jane in the lead. The wind pushed back against her, sending sand and sea spray into her eyes. Star ducked her head, shielding her face with her forelock as best she could. It was a long, miserable night for the Sand Pounders and their horses.

Though still dark, Jane knew the sun would soon rise in the east.

"Let's make one last patrol of the north beach then call it a night," Stephan said.

"Best idea you've ever had," Jane said as she brushed her wet hair out of her eyes. "I'll lead."

As Jane and Star neared the rocky cliffs that separated Lincoln City from Neskowin, Jane spotted a dark object on the sand just at the water's edge. The waves covered it as they came in, exposing it as they receded. She pulled out her binoculars and looked more closely, but in the surrounding darkness, it was impossible to determine what it was.

As she rode closer, a flash of lightning illuminated the beach all around her. A body. Jane was sure of it. She nudged Star into a canter. As they drew near, Star's ears pricked forward and she came to a sudden stop, nearly throwing Jane out of the saddle.

Lying on the beach, tangled in a web of ropes and wood, was a woman's body!

19

October 1942

The wild pounding of the sea continued as Jane jumped from her horse, the weight of the radio strapped to her back causing her to stumble and nearly fall. She made her way through the waves to the body. Bending down, she pulled with all her strength but couldn't dislodge the body from the flotsam around it. Turning, she splashed back through the churning water to Star and pulled a rope from her saddle bag. Tying one end to her saddle, she wound the other end around the woman's body. "Step back, Star. Step back." At first the horse hesitated, spooked by the wild waves swirling around her legs. "Step back, girl. Step back," Jane yelled over the howling wind.

Slowly, Star stepped back, dragging the body with her.

As soon as Jane was able to get the body clear of the waves, she rolled it over with trembling hands. She noticed scrapes on the skin through patches of torn clothing. As Jane examined the body, her panic soon resigned to confusion. Clearly the woman was dead but where did she come from?

Stephan came galloping up the beach to help. "John, what is it?" he shouted over a clap of thunder.

"Oh, Stephan, this woman is dead," Jane said as she untied the rope she had wrapped around the woman to pull her from the breakers. She stood on the wet sand, her clothes dripping, looking in all directions. Her teeth chattered from the cold. "B-but I c-can't figure out where she c-came from."

"There," Stephan said, pointing out to sea.

Jane looked in the direction her partner was pointing, toward where the cliffs jutted out into the ocean. A distress signal was piercing the darkness. Morse code for S-O-S flashed, then went dark, then flashed again.

"I'm c-calling in," she said, shrugging off her pack that held the radio. She called the Beach Patrol Station. "A ship has been spotted. Run aground on the cliffs at the north end of Lincoln City Beach. It might be the enemy," Jane said breathlessly into the microphone. Immediately, search parties on foot and in boats were dispatched to the area. Jane and

Stephan waited for help. The wind and rain still relentless, they huddled against their horses.

One small boat from the Coast Guard Station in Tillamook Bay arrived first and spotted a hapless freighter marooned against the rocky cliffs. Even in the darkness of the storm, the men on board the coast guard vessel could see sailors on board, signaling for help. But the waves were too rough to even attempt a sea rescue.

Jane received a call. "The ship has been spotted. Run aground on those cliffs," Jane said to Stephan after communicating with the Station. "We need to climb the rocks and see what we can do to help."

Stephan reached into his saddle bag. "The only rescue equipment we have are these ropes and some first aid supplies."

"The ropes will have to do. Let's bring them."

Strapping their guns to their backs and the ropes over their shoulders, the two Sand Pounders ran to the cliff. The erstwhile equestrians turned into rock climbers and started scaling the face of the cliff. Finding one foothold and handhold at a time, Jane and Stephan slowly worked their way up the slippery, nearly vertical wall of stone. Jane felt the wind and rain pummel her from all sides. Her fingers ached from the cold. Her boots were stiff and proved to be unsuitable for climbing. She paused and rested her cheek against the rock. She felt her heart pounding in her chest as cold beads of sweat mixed with the rain.

"You okay?" she heard Stephan say from above. She looked up to see her partner already at the top. He was on his stomach, his arm reaching down to her.

Too tired to respond, she took a deep breath and moved one foot up until she found a foothold. Pushing up with all the strength she could muster, she reached for his hand.

"Thanks, Stephan," Jane said as he pulled her over the lip of the ledge.

"No problem. That wasn't easy."

Safely on top of the ridge, they hurried toward the point and cautiously worked their way out to the precipitous edge. Lying side by side on their stomachs, they looked down. The wind-blown waves had wedged the freighter against the cliff, and it was slowly settling over on its side.

"What kind of ship is that?" Jane shouted over the wind.

"It looks like a freighter of some sort."

"Is it Japanese?" Jane said, her breath bursting in and out in fear and cold. Stephan pulled out his binoculars.

"No, look," he said, handing her the glasses. "Those people aren't Japanese."

Jane looked through the glasses at the seamen on board. She counted forty-five men and eight women on board the ship. They were in grave danger. Handing the binoculars back she said, "Look at the lifeboat dangling off the side, it's broken to bits. Now I know where that woman tangled in the rope and boards came from."

"Is it safe for us to contact them, do you think?   Let them know we're here?" Stephan asked, replacing the binoculars in their case.

"We might as well. They're the ones in danger, not us."

"Hello! Hello down there!" Stephan yelled through cupped hands.

The people on the ship looked up and began waving their arms and shouting back.

Jane couldn't understand a word.

"Russian. They're speaking Russian," Stephan said.

Jane looked askance. "How do you know that?"

"I rode in a clinic with a Russian Olympic Team member. I recognize it."

"Can you answer them?"

Stephan snorted. "I didn't say I can speak it."

"Well, let's start a rescue operation and hope they catch on," Jane said, pulling her rope off her shoulder and reaching for Stephan's. "The only thing I can think of is to lower these ropes and let them climb up. I don't feel we have time to wait around for help."

The two Sand Pounders tied their ropes together and heaved their line over the edge. In frustration, they watched as the rope fell just short of the sailors.

"I have an idea," Jane said in a moment of inspiration. She unlaced her belt and her shoelaces. Stephan caught on immediately and unlaced his as well. They attached the belts and laces to the end and lowered the rope again. This time, the seamen grabbed the line and attached a heavier cable from their ship.

"They're brilliant," Jane said as she and Stephan pulled up their makeshift rope, with the heavy line attached. "Now we have enough rope to secure it to those trees over there." Stepan grabbed the ship's rope and ran toward a clump of gnarled, wind-blown trees.

"Hurry, Stephan, the ship keeps shifting! Those people don't have much time." Jane felt her heart pounding.

"Got it," Stephan said as he returned to the edge of the cliff. Jane and Stephan started motioning for the seamen to climb up.

One by one, everyone on board the ship climbed up the rope, hand reaching over hand as their feet searched for footholds on the rock face. The angry black clouds threatened them from above, the snarling waves and vicious rocks from below. When they reached the top, they collapsed, panting from both fear and exertion. Just as the captain, the last seaman on the freighter, grabbed the rope, the ship twisted and rolled. A giant wave crashed over the stern. He jumped off, hanging onto the hawser as his men pulled him up.

By the time all the crew were on the headland, several more Sand Pounders and Coast Guardsmen arrived on the beach. The sky was getting lighter and the wind and rain, mercifully, had calmed a bit.

Stephan pulled the rope up as he turned to Jane. "Well, as hard as it is to believe, they all got up here. Now, how do we get them down?"

"Rappel," Jane said.

"Rappel? Do you know how to do that?"

"Not exactly, but I've seen it done. Do you know how?"

"Nope. Show jumping is my sport, remember."

Jane smiled. "Okay, I'll go first to demonstrate."

Using the ropes and the cable, Jane and Stephan set up two rappel lines. As Jane stood at the edge of the cliff, her back to the beach, she paused to calm her nerves. One of the Russians held up his hand and approached her. Nodding and smiling, he picked up the other rope. Turning, he pushed off. Jane turned her head and watched him slide down the rope, using his legs to push off the cliff. Taking a deep breath, she followed.

Stephan remained on top and helped the tired and frightened sailors rappel down the cliff to waiting arms. Trucks were ready to carry them to the warmth and safety of the Coast Guard Station.

An hour later, the sun now up, turning the clouds a soft gray, Jane and Stephan stood beside their horses and watched the trucks pull away.

"You were amazing up there, John," Stephan said, pounding Jane on the back.

Jane choked on a cough. She dropped her chin and looked down at their lace-less boots. "I wouldn't have made it to the top if it hadn't been for you."

"Oh, poppycock. You had it made."

Jane shook her head. "I'm not as strong as I thought I was," she whispered.

"You may not be the strongest Sand Pounder, but you're probably the smartest," Stephan said. "What do ya say we call it a night?"

Jane looked around. "Looks like day to me," she said with a smirk.

20

November 1942

The sailors who had been rescued were taken to the Coast Guard Station in Garibaldi where the Sand Pounders had trained. Representatives from the Navy arrived to question them.

A few days later, Jane and Stephan received a visit from the Commander.

"Sand Pounders Morris and Peters, I have come to commend you for your excellent work rescuing the sailors from what could have been a great tragedy. Your quick thinking and heroic actions saved many lives."

"Thank you, Commander," Stephan said. "John really gets all the credit. I just did what he told me to do."

"Stephan and I worked as a team, the way we are supposed to, Sir," Jane said. Stephan smiled at Jane.

"Sir, can you tell us what you have discovered about the ship and its crew?" Stephan asked.

"We have learned that, just as you suspected, they were aboard a Russian freighter. Having lost its bearings during the storm, it headed inland, intent on reaching the port in Astoria. They didn't realize the port at the mouth of the Columbia River was still eighty-five miles to the north." The Commander lifted his cap and ran his fingers through his hair before continuing. "The Navy was curious to find out if they had seen any Japanese submarines in the area, to which they replied they had not. That doesn't mean we don't need to remain vigilant. The Japanese may very well have been aware of their presence and avoided detection."

For the next two months, the four Sand Pounders in Lincoln City established a comfortable routine while never letting down their guard. They kept their eyes peeled on the horizon in search of enemy ships. On occasion, they questioned people on the beach who seemed out of place. Their most frequent task seemed to be putting out campfires left by the occasional local who wanted nothing more than to roast a few marshmallows.

Yet, they gained encouragement from the thought that their very presence might well be what was preventing an invasion.

Over the great waters, however, the war raged on.

One December day, Jeannie came to the cabin at Devils Lake in the late afternoon to deliver letters. As she handed the envelope to Jane, Stephan entered the room. "And who is this?" she asked.

"Hello," said Stephan, immediately melting Jeannie with one of his winning smiles. "I'm Stephan Peters. And you are . . .?"

"I-I-I'm Ja . . . John's friend, Jeannie," she said, her face blushing brightly even in the dimly lit room.

"Are you a horsewoman?" Stephan asked, ignoring her discomfort.

"Yes . . . but not nearly as good as John."

"Nor am I," he said, giving Jane a slap on the back.

Shaking her head, Jane turned to Jeannie. "Thanks for bringing these letters, Jeannie. I'm sure you're in a hurry to get home."

"Oh, I have plenty of time," Jeannie said, still eyeing Stephan.

"I'm sure you need to get home," Jane whispered under her breath as she pulled her friend toward the door.

Jeannie looked back over her shoulder. "Nice to meet you, Stephan. I guess I'm going now."

Outside and out of earshot, Jeannie said, "Wow. Is that your partner?"

"Yes," Jane said, trying to act nonchalant.

"No wonder you want to be a Sand Pounder," Jeannie said.

"We work together. That's all there is to it."

"Maybe I need to come visit you more often, then," Jeannie added with a grin as she lifted her hand and flipped her hair.

"Jeannie!"

"Just kidding."

21

December 1942

With Jeannie safely on her way home, Jane retreated to her bunk to read her letters.

There was a letter from her brother, her grandmother, and Thomas Kato.

She unfolded the letter from her brother first. She immediately noticed the places in the letter that had been censored by the Navy to keep locations a secret. She noticed that it had been written four months previously.

August 1, 1942

Dear Jane,

I lay in bed at night with tears wetting my pillow. It is so hard to be away from

my home and family. War is such a
terrible thing. My nightmares wake me at
night . . . at least the nights I get to sleep.
I have watched dear friends suffer and
die in the battle of ███████████ I am so
thankful that you do not have to be doing
what I am doing. I rarely get off the ship
so I haven't seen much of the world as I
once thought I would. I have a chance to
go to shore at ███████████████ so I will be
able to mail this letter. Right after I get
on   board,   we   will   set   sail   for
███████████████ on a mission that will keep
us at sea for many weeks. My only joy is
thinking of you, Grandma, and Aunt Molly
safe at home. Keep me in your prayers. I
need them.

   Your devoted brother,
   Luke

Jane felt the tears overflow and trickle down
her cheeks. She folded the letter, got up, set it
on her dresser, and went into the bathroom to
wash her face.

"John, you ready for our patrol?" Stephan called through the door.

Jane cleared her throat. "I'll be right out," she called. She grabbed some toilet paper and blew her nose. Flushing the tissue down the toilet she lifted her chin and stepped out of the room.

The evening threatened to be the precursor to a cold night. The wind blew and the ocean spit its foam at them as Jane and Stephan patrolled both sides of D River. Jane kept her binoculars trained on the heaving ocean as she rode along. Star, well-acquainted with the routine by now, needed little direction. Jane's thoughts kept returning to her brother's letter and her heart ached. She wished she could tell him that she was doing all she could to defend their country and put an end to the war. But she dared not reveal her secret to anyone. Only her grandmother and Jeannie knew what she was hiding.

The hours dragged on, tedious and tiring.

When, at last, Stephan turned back and told her it was time to go in, she was too weary to even respond. She merely turned Star around and let her horse follow Big Bay up the trail they used to get back to the little house.

Chip and Tim were already in the corral tacking up their horses when Jane and Stephan arrived.

"Pretty lousy day for a ride, I'd say," Tim said, wrapping his rain coat tightly around him.

Jane merely nodded, letting the rain drip off her short curls and into her eyes. She dismounted. Turning to Stephan, she said, "I"ll take care of the horses. You go heat up some coffee."

"Deal," Stephan said, handing her the reins to Big Bay.

A half hour later, Jane stepped up on the wooden porch, stomped the mud off her boots and opened the front foor.

Stephan stood in the center of the room. In his hand he held a letter—Luke's letter. "Jane?" was all he said.

Jane's body stiffened. She felt blood rush to her face. "You got into my private letter?" she hissed between clenched teeth.

"The window was open and the wind blew it onto the floor. I merely picked it up. I'm sorry. I didn't mean to pry."

Jane dropped to her knees and started weeping.

Stephan remained standing, cross-armed, looking down at her with an arched brow. He said nothing more, only waited for Jane to respond.

Sniffling and wiping her nose on her sleeve, Jane let out a moan.

"You're a *girl*?"

Jane nodded.

Stephan began pacing the room. "Well, that explains a lot, now that I think about it." He stopped and looked down at her. "To tell you the truth, I feel pretty stupid." He bent down and helped her stand. He led her over to the couch. They both sat.

Stephan breathed out a loud sigh. Jane bit her lip. For a time, only the wind, trying to work its way inside the little house, made a sound.

Jane sniffed. "So, what are you going to do?"

"Me? I don't see why I should do anything. You're the best Sand Pounder we've got."

Jane's eyes popped open, and her jaw dropped. "Y-y-you're not going to turn me in?" she stuttered.

"Why should I? If I do that, they'll send you home and send me a new partner. I don't want a new partner."

Jane threw her arms around Stephan's neck and buried her face in his chest. "Oh, thank you, thank you. You're the best partner anyone ever had."

Stephan held his arms out then hesitantly wrapped them around her as she cried. "Can I still call you 'John?'" he said with a chuckle.

22

December 1942

Later in the day of "the great discovery," as Stephan referred to finding out about Jane's true identity, Jane found time to read her other letters.

Her grandmother's letter was full of news about the townspeople and the things they were doing to help with the war effort. Grandmother and Aunt Molly's "Victory Garden" had produced enough vegetables for them to preserve for the winter with enough extra to share with neighbors. Aunt Molly had taken on the job of washing the aluminum foil since it was difficult to purchase. Grandmother had been unable to purchase sugar without the use of government-issued coupons since the spring, but she was learning to bake using applesauce for a sweetener. Vouchers for coffee were just introduced this month. Since Grandmother never drank coffee, she was trading those coupons with neighbors for other items.

Picturing Grandmother and Aunt Molly in their little house, washing the aluminum foil made her smile.

She set the letter aside and picked up the letter from Thomas.

November 10, 1942

Dear Jane,

How are you doing? Are you attending college? Perhaps at the Oregon State College Extension school? Or are you working? I haven't heard from you since the summer so I'm sure you have a lot going on.

Life in Tule Lake is a lot better since the weather has cooled. It was a hot, dry, miserable summer to be sure, but we are past that now.

My father has been put in charge of the mess hall for the "Official Family." They are a Caucasian family that is in charge of the camp. I don't know why they picked him, as his experience with food has been limited to owning a fish market. But he is learning, and they seem to like his cooking. They even issued him a car, so he gets to leave the camp to purchase food. He actually gets paid as much as the camp doctor: $19 a month. Our family gets to enjoy the leftovers, so we are eating better than most.

There are still days when I am so angry at the government, I entertain the idea of running away. But I don't know where I would go. I have heard of Japanese prisoners (yes, in my mind we are prisoners!) who have been shot and killed trying to escape. At another camp, one couple actually got shot just for walking too close to the fence.

I'm sorry to keep complaining. It is hard to keep a positive attitude as days become weeks and weeks become months, yet there is no change in sight.

Appreciate your freedom. You never know when it might be taken away.

Your friend,
Thomas Kato

Jane set the letter down. Lifting her chin, she stared across the room at nothing in particular. Her lips pressed into a thin line. Her hands formed fists, her nails biting into her palm. She forced herself to slow her breathing as she stood and walked to the kitchen to get a drink of water.

Still, her heart pounded in her chest. It all seemed so wrong, yet what could she do?

The day of the great discovery was the turning point for Jane and Stephan. Their partnership grew closer with each passing day. It was as though the secret they kept served to bind them together. The one difference Jane noticed was that Stephan didn't like being as far away from her when they were on patrol. When a wintertime storm sent strong wind, sheets of rain, and wild waves over the sand, Jane turned to find Stephan right behind her instead of the recommended hundred yards back.

"What are you doing?" she shouted over the pounding of the waves.

"Nothing."

"Why are you right on Star's tail?"

"Big Bay and I just want to make sure you're okay," Stephan said.

"Well get back where you belong. We have a job to do," Jane said. She turned forward. She couldn't help but smile as a warm feeling filled her chest.

23

January 1943

January 1943 arrived. The war continued and Jane could not tell if the United States and its allies were winning or not. Though information was spotty and often tainted to keep Americans from getting discouraged, some news got through. The Battle of Guadalcanal started on August 7, 1942, and was still going on. Jane listened for any news of the battle as it was initially a naval operation that had become a land battle. She worried constantly about her brother. The Navy sent amphibious vehicles on land and seized a strategic airfield. It was the first major land offensive against the Japanese and was proving to be both long and bloody. Jane wondered if Luke was involved in this battle. She had no way of knowing for sure.

At the end of the month, another news story appeared. A major event took place on the European side of the war on January 27th. The VIII Bomber Command dispatched ninety-one B-17s and B-24s to attack the U-Boat construction yards at Wilhelmshaven, Germany. This was the first bombing attack on Germany of the war.

Tensions along the American coast increased, and the locals in the area where Jane and Stephan patrolled were more grateful than ever for the presence of the Sand Pounders. Freshly baked loaves of bread and home-canned food often appeared on their porch.

Jane and Stephan continued to alternate with Tim and Chip as to which team covered the beaches at night, and which team took the day shift. As can be expected, the day shift, even in the rain, was much more pleasant than the night.

Jane and Stephan were on their first night of the shift change. They had been on their horses all day but returned to the house just long enough to feed and water them. They grabbed something to eat for themselves before heading back to the beach.

"I'll take the lead this time," Jane said. "And you don't have to be on Star's heels. We'll be fine."

"Yes ma'am," Stephan said, giving her a salute with his right hand.

"You better not call me that," Jane said with a twinkle in her eye. "Someone might hear you."

Jane tapped her calves against Star's sides and started down the beach at a trot.

The night got colder and darker. No moon glowed behind the clouds. Jane was ahead of Stephan by several minutes of trotting. The waves crashed against the shore. Over the sound of the waves, Jane heard a popping sound. She pulled out her binoculars and searched out to sea, the direction from which the odd sound had come. She stopped Star and looked again. She couldn't see anything, especially not something that would make a popping sound. Reaching the end of the beach, she turned around and headed north, approaching Stephan on her way. Stopping her horse, she said, "Did you hear that popping sound?"

"I did. It sounded like gunshots, but I couldn't tell where it was coming from."

"Let's keep our eyes peeled," Jane said as she rode off.

"John."

Jane stopped and looked back at Stephan.

"Be careful, okay?"

Jane smiled. "I will. Don't worry about me." She turned back. A smile crossed her face.

Over the next hour Jane rode to the north end of the beach, turned, and headed back south. Star splashed across D River, her hooves making sucking sounds in the wet sand.

A sudden movement at the edge of the water caught her eye. In the darkness it was difficult to tell what it was, but Jane guessed it was a sea lion coming ashore. She watched it lift its bulky body then flop itself forward. It slowly worked its way out of the waves and onto the wet sand. Jane pulled out her binoculars. Twisting the knobs, she focused on the creature. Dread crept through her, clawing its way up her spine. What she was looking at was no sea lion. It was a person.

She lowered her binoculars and squinted. She turned and looked back for Stephan. He was still quite a ways back. Lifting the binoculars, she looked again. The person was not moving.

She put Star into a canter and ran up the beach. As they approached, Star spooked at the sudden appearance of something strange on the beach, whirling to one side. Jane got the mare under control and dismounted. She pulled her rifle from its holder and aimed it at the body.

Cautiously, she approached the figure lying in the sand. She started to reach down when it moaned. She jumped back, her heart in her throat.

"H-hello. I'm here to help you," she said, her teeth chattering. "W-who are you?"

The person moaned again, and Jane noticed a dark streak on the sand extending to the water. Blood.

She dropped her gun and knelt beside the body. "You're hurt. Let me help you."

The person lifted his head and Jane gasped. Japanese! She struggled to swallow the tingle of nausea in her throat. She stayed where she was, kneeling in the sand, gawking at him as he stared back at her.

The man struggled to speak. "I-I'm an American citizen . . . escaped . . . submarine . . . shot me." His attempt at talking turned into a coughing fit. He moaned again and his head dropped back to the sand.

Just then, Stephan came cantering up, his horse sliding to a stop. He jumped off Big Bay. "John, what is it?"

Jane looked up at Stephan. "He's Japanese."

Stephan pulled his gun out and aimed it at the prone body.

Jane jumped up, extending her arms and blocking Stephan's aim. Fearful determination was etched across her face. "No, Stephan! He said he's an American citizen, a Japanese American, like my neighbors who were sent away to an internment camp. It sounded like he escaped from a sub and they shot him."

Lowering his gun, Stephan said, "And you believe him?"

"Well, look at the blood. Somebody shot him."

"So, let's call this in," he said, reaching for the radio strapped to his back.

Jane lowered her arms and planted her fists on her hips. Her thoughts were on the Katos. "I don't want to."

"What? What are you talking about?"

"I want to help him get better. Then we can decide what to do."

"You want to aide the enemy?" Stephan said, pacing back and forth, his eyes glued to the body.

"He's not the enemy if he's an American citizen as he claimed."

"Look at his uniform . . . he's dressed like a Japanese sailor. He could have just been telling you a story to sneak ashore."

Jane nodded. "It could have been, but I don't think so. He sounded American, not Japanese."

Stephan rubbed his temples. He stopped pacing and faced Jane. "Jane, he's probably one of the enemy. We can't just let him go."

"I don't plan to let him go."

"Well, what do you suggest?"

"He needs medical help."

"That's pretty obvious."

"Let's take him to Doc."

Stephan removed his cap and ran his fingers through his hair. He bit his lip and shook his head. "I don't think this is a good idea. You're suggesting we harbor an enemy."

"We don't know that he *is* an enemy!" Jane shouted, frustration rising within her.

"But we don't know that he isn't!" Stephan shouted back with equal frustration in his voice.

Jane took a deep breath to calm her nerves. Lowering her voice, she pleaded, "Stephan, please. If we turn him in, he'll be treated like a prisoner of war, maybe even killed. If we take him to Doc and get him well, we can sort this out. Maybe he *is* an enemy, but what if he told me the truth?"

Stephan kicked at the sand. "I don't know. I just don't know," he said, his face taut, his hands curled into fists.

Jane reached out, her hand trembling, and touched his arm. "Let's 'harbor' him, as you say, just long enough to find out what's going on. If he's a Japanese soldier, I promise I'll be the first to turn him in."

Stephan looked into her pleading eyes for a long minute. Then he offered a slight nod of his head.

Jane grinned and leaned over and kissed him on the cheek. Surprised at her response she quickly stepped back. Her hands flew over her hasty lips, her body rigid with embarrassment.

Stephan smiled. "That made this almost worth it."

24

January 1943

D r. Dirksen and his wife were jarred awake by a loud pounding on their door. Startled, they both sat up in the darkness of their room. Dr. Dirksen reached over and turned on the bedside lamp. Melanie clutched the blankets under her chin and trembled.

"W-who is it?" she stuttered.

"Probably someone needing a doctor. I'll go check," Doc said.

Wrapping himself in a robe, Doc opened the front door a crack. Peeking through the narrow opening, he saw a Sand Pounder.

"Doc," Jane said, her breathing heavy. "I need your help."

"John, what's the matter?" Doc said, flinging the door wide.

"A man has been shot."

"Shot? Where is he?"

Jane turned around and pointed at Star. Draped over Star's saddle was a dark figure.

Dr. Dirksen pushed his way past Jane and approached the horse. "Help me get him inside," he said to Jane. They pulled the injured man down. The man groaned as they did so. "He's alive, at least," Doc said.

Jane clenched her teeth as she held onto the man's legs. Her muscles, already tired from the night's ordeal, cried in complaint. Struggling across the slippery walkway, the two of them managed to get the limp body in the house.

"Lay him across the dining room table," Doc said, leading the way to the dining room.

Once the injured man was on the table, Doc turned on the overhead light and returned to examine the body. As he bent over to look at his face, Doc gasped, then jumped back in shock. "He's Japanese!"

"Yes," Jane said, rubbing the back of her neck.

Doc cast her a questioning look.

"Stephan and I found him on the beach. He washed ashore. He's been shot."

Doc shook his head and pursed his lips, letting out a loud breath. He turned back to the man and started searching for injuries. He rolled him over on his stomach. On his back, he found two bullet holes, one in a shoulder and the other in a hip. "Well, he might be lucky. The frigid salt water stemmed the loss of blood. Let's get these bullets out."

For the next hour, Dr. Dirksen worked to carefully remove the bullets. Melanie helped by heating clean rags to dress the wounds. The man remained unconscious, unaware of what was happening to him.

After Doc finished bandaging the wounds and dressing the man in a clean, dry gown, he, his wife, and Jane carried the near-lifeless body to a spare bedroom.

Melanie disappeared into the kitchen to boil some water for tea.

"Come sit down in the living room, John," Doc said.

Jane quietly obeyed, sitting in the middle of the couch. Clasping her hands in her lap, she looked up at her kind neighbor, her eyes beseeching.

"Why don't you tell me what happened tonight," he said, taking a chair and placing it in front of her. Melanie entered the room and handed each of them a welcome cup of hot tea.

Jane took the proffered cup and smiled at Melanie in acknowledgement.

Doc took a sip from his cup and waited, his eyes never leaving Jane.

Slowly, hesitantly, Jane told the story of what had transpired, including the argument she had with Stephan. She ended by saying, "After Stephan and I managed to get him on Star's back,

I led her here while Stephan finished our patrol assignment by himself."

Doc brought one hand up to cover his mouth, his fingers curling around his chin. He looked down at his teacup and said nothing for quite a while.

Jane took another sip of her now-cooled tea. Leaning forward, she set the cup on the coffee table. She could hear the ticking of the grandfather clock behind her.

Doc looked up. "You said he told you he was an American citizen?"

Jane bit her lip and nodded.

"You believe he escaped from a Japanese sub?"

Jane nodded again.

Doc stood and paced the room. He scratched his head and breathed deeply, letting out the air in a huff. "Well, we have quite a problem on our hands."

"I'm sorry to bring you into this. I just didn't know where else to turn," Jane said, wringing her hands.

"It is my responsibility to save lives. But now what do I do? What is my responsibility now?" he said, rubbing his temples with both hands.

"Do you think he will live?"

"Too soon to tell. It depends on how strong he is."

Melanie jumped in. "Well, I think we should wait until he can tell us his side of the story before we do anything."

25

January 1943

Jane led Star back to the corral. The sun was up, though mostly covered by a blanket of clouds. She shuffled along in front of her horse, frequently getting nudged by Star's muzzle. "I know. You're as tired and hungry as I am," she said, looking down at her feet as they moved along the muddy road as though of their own volition.

Jane untacked Star, noticing that Big Bay was happily munching on hay in the corral. He nickered at them as Jane opened the wobbly, make-shift gate and put Star inside the enclosure. She threw more hay over the fence and went inside.

The house was quiet. The covered windows blocked any light from the outside. Only a single lightbulb over the kitchen sink lit the room. Jane went to the old, rusty refrigerator and pulled out some apple juice, a gift from a neighbor. She sat down and sliced some bread.

After eating her meager meal, she went into the bunk room. Stephan's body formed a mound on the top bunk.

"Well, what happened?"

Jane jumped. "I thought you were asleep."

"Can't sleep. I'm dead tired but I can't sleep. Worrying too much."

"Doc removed two bullets and bandaged him up. Too soon to tell if he'll make it or not."

"Might be better if he doesn't," Stephan mumbled.

Jane nodded. "Yeah. I know what you mean by that."

After changing in the bathroom, Jane returned to the little room and collapsed on her bunk. "What did you say to Tim and Chip?"

"I told them you were sick and went to see Doc."

Jane nodded. "Good thinking."

"I don't like lying."

"I know. Me neither." She sat up in her bed. "Stephan?"

"Yes?"

"Thank you. I don't know if we did the right thing or not. I guess only time will tell. But I appreciate your support."

Stephan mumbled something unintelligible. Jane smiled and lay back down. Sleep overtook her.

The front door banged behind them as Tim and Chip entered the house. "Hey Stephan, are you going out?" Tim yelled from the front room.

Stephan sat up and dropped down from his bunk. "Yeah. Just overslept," he said, rubbing his eyes.

"How's John doing?" Chip said, entering the room.

Jane threw back her covers and started to stand up.

"Whoa partner. Why don't you just stay where you are?" Chip said. "I'll take your shift for you."

"I appreciate that, but I can do it," Jane said.

"What did Doc give you?" Chip asked.

"Ummm," she hesitated as she tried to figure out a way around the question. "He took care of me really well. I feel fine, now."

"Well, cowboy, that's good to hear but are you sure you don't need to take it easy today?"

"No, Chip. Thank you, but I'm fine, really," Jane said, grabbing her uniform and heading for the bathroom.

"Your horse has been fed," he called after her.

Puffy clouds glowed orange, reflecting the sunset, as Stephan and Jane rode toward the beach. Halfway up the shore of D River, Jane stopped her horse.

Stephan came up beside her. "What is it?"

"I want to check on Doc and the sailor before I start the patrol."

"Okay."

"You go ahead," Jane said, pulling gloves out of her pocket and working her hands into them.

"I'll come with you."

Jane looked askance. "You will?"

"I'm in this, too, you know," Stephan said, turning Big Bay around on the narrow path.

Jane and Stephan trotted past their little house. Chip and Tim's horses called out to them as they passed. It was getting dark and, due to blackout instructions, no porch lights offered a welcome. No warm windows glowed. Everything was quiet and ominous as they approached Doc's house. They tied their horses to the fence that ran across the front of his yard and stepped up to the door.

Jane reached up and rapped her gloved knuckles on the front door. She heard movement from inside and soon the door opened slightly.

"Hi, Doc," Jane said. "Stephan is with me. We came to check on the patient."

"Come in," Doc said. "I was hoping that was you."

"Is he doing alright?"

"He's conscious. Very weak. But he seems to be doing as well as can be expected."

"Has he said anything?" Stephan asked, taking off his cap and twisting the rim in his hands.

"Not yet. Give him time. He'll open up."

"Are you in need of anything?" Jane asked.

Doc shook his head. "The wife and I are pretty self-sufficient, but I'll let you know if we do."

"We'll come back tomorrow to check on him," Jane added, placing a hand on Doc's arm.

Jane and Stephan headed out into the night, mounted their horses, and rode to the beach. As she rode along, the rhythmic four-beat walk of her horse brought comfort and she reached down to rub Star's neck. Numerous thoughts ran through her mind. She didn't know if she was relieved that the sailor seemed to be getting better or not. She didn't know what that would mean for him or for her . . . or for Stephan. She knew one thing; she would not let Stephan take the blame for any of this.

26

February 1943

The next day and for a few days thereafter, word reached the Lincoln City Sand Pounders that a submarine had been spotted off the Oregon Coast by one of the blimps from Tillamook. The blimp was tracking its movements. The Sand Pounders were warned to be on high alert and report anything suspicious. While Stephan remained quiet, Jane could feel the tension radiating from his every movement. Even Big Bay seemed to sense it, dancing around and spooking at the slightest provocation.

A week after finding the injured sailor, Jane visited Doc and Melanie early in the morning. She was surprised to find the stranger sitting up in bed when she peeked in the room. A small lamp glowed from atop a bedside table.

Jane entered the room. "Hello," Jane said, feeling surprisingly timid.

"Hello," the man said in a clear American accent. "Are you the one Doc told me about? The one to whom I owe my life?"

Jane blushed. "Well, I'm the one who found you on the beach. It's Doc who really saved your life."

"Why didn't you finish me off?" he asked, his dark, narrow eyes imploring.

"You said you were an American."

"I did?" He knotted his eyebrows and looked toward the covered window. "I don't remember." He turned back and looked at her. "Did I say anything else?" he said, shifting in the bed to find a more comfortable position.

"Not much before you passed out. You did say you came from a submarine, and they had shot you."

He looked down at his hands as they twisted the sheet. By this time, Doc had entered the room. The older man reached for a chair and offered it to Jane. Jane sat, leaned forward, and rested her elbows on her knees.

"Do you feel strong enough to tell me what happened?" Jane asked.

"What do you want to know?"

"Well . . . everything. But let's start with your name."

"My name is Brian Kikomoto."

"Brian is an American name."

"Yes. I was born in Placerville, California. My relatives arrived with a group of Japanese in an area called Gold Hill in 1869. They were part of the group that built the Wakamatsu Tea and Silk Farm Colony. While the colony only survived for two years, my ancestors stayed in the area working farms and starting businesses. I am a fourth-generation American."

Jane felt her muscles get tight and her hands ball into fists. She pursed her lips and tilted her head to one side. Raising her eyebrows, she said, "If what you say is true, why were you on a Japanese submarine off our shores?"

"First, you must believe me. What I said is completely true." He shifted in his bed again, trying to get comfortable. Doc brought him a glass of water and a pain pill. Jane waited.

After swallowing the pill, Brian continued. "I wanted to learn more about my Japanese heritage, so I went to Japan over three years ago to study at Tokyo University. I was living with a distant cousin and going to school when the war broke out. One night, military officers came to my door and conscripted me into the Navy. They gave me no choice."

Jane felt her heart race. "You were forced into the army to fight your own country?"

"They didn't care where I was from. They needed bodies."

"So, you ended up on a Japanese submarine off the coast of Oregon?" Doc said.

Jane looked at Doc, trying to read his thoughts. His eyes looked sympathetic, not skeptical. She turned back to Brian.

"Tell me what happened before I found you on the beach."

"Yes, sir," Brian said. "You may have heard about the attempted attack in 1942 by a Japanese pilot in a submarine-based floatplane. He tried to start a fire around the town of Brookings, Oregon by dropping incendiary devices over the forest."

Jane and Doc nodded. Jane had been told about this event during her coast guard training . . . another reason the Sand Pounders were so desperately needed.

"Well, I was supposed to do the same thing to the forests east of here."

Jane's eyes opened wide. "How?"

"The submarine surfaced, and the floatplane was disengaged. But instead of getting into the plane, I jumped ship when I thought the other sailors were busy getting the plane ready. I'm a strong swimmer—a lifeguard, I thought I could make it to shore." Shaking his head, he added, "In my desperation, I guess I didn't anticipate how cold the water is and how strong the currents are this far north."

"But they saw you go overboard," Jane said, understanding dawning.

Brian nodded. "I guess it wasn't such a good plan. They could have killed me . . . would have killed me if it weren't for you."

Jane stood and patted him on the hand. She turned to Doc. "Can you come to the other room with me, Doc?"

Doc stood and followed her out of the bedroom and into the living room.

Lowering her voice to a whisper, she said, "Do you believe him?"

"Yes. I must say I do," Doc said. "Do you?"

"I don't know. I think so. If what he says is true, I don't know what to do about it."

"I'll leave that to you. I'm just the doctor." Patting Jane's shoulder, Doc added, "I'm doing my job. Now you get to do yours."

Jane left the house and stepped into the misty morning, so typical of Oregon winters. She walked down the road, her head down, deep in thought. Star's nicker brought her back to the present. She went into the corral where Star was lying on the sand under the makeshift shelter the Sand Pounders had built out of available scraps of lumber and tin.

"Hi, girl," Jane said as she sat next to the mare's curled-up front legs. "Feels good to get off your feet, doesn't it?" She stroked Star's neck and ran her fingers through her mane. She leaned against the horse's strong shoulder, finding solace in the mare's presence.

Jane remained there, her mind a whirl of thoughts, her stomach twisted. She pulled her knees to her chin and rubbed her hands up and down her pant legs. A shiver ran through her body. Star wrapped her neck around and placed her muzzle on Jane's arm. Just as the sun gradually rises and brings light to the day, Jane's mind was illuminated. She knew exactly what she needed to do.

Before retiring to her bunk, Jane wrote a letter to Thomas Kato and placed a call to her friend Jeannie.

27

February 1943

Eleanor Roosevelt, the President's wife, took a tour of England in 1942 to see how they were handling the strain the war was creating on the food supply. While there, she met with members of the Women's Land Army about their work in agriculture. She was impressed with the results the English women had shown in producing agricultural products. She returned to her homeland and began lobbying for a similar system to be put in place in the U.S. Initially, she met with resistance from the USDA, but as more and more men were needed to join the fighting in the long and exhausting war, it became obvious that women were needed not just in the factories but on the farms as well.

In 1943, Congress passed the Emergency Farm Labor Program, creating the Women's Land Army of America, dubbed the WLAA.

A short time later, Jeannie wrote Jane a letter and told her friend how much she admired her efforts, while slipping in a line about her handsome partner. She wrote that she had decided to join the WLAA. She was working on one of the many dairy farms around Tillamook. She admitted that cows were not as wonderful as horses, but she enjoyed working with animals all the same.

Jane hoped that with Jeannie working on a dairy farm, she would be in a position to help with her plan. Stephan was sleeping in the other room, so Jane knew it was a good time to use the telephone. Now she was standing in the kitchen of their little house with the phone to her ear. She dialed Jeannie's parents' number and hoped that no one on the party line would pick up and listen. She impatiently drummed her fingers on the Formica top of the table as the phone on the other end rang. She pictured it hanging on the kitchen wall of Jeannie's house, a house she hadn't seen for more than half a year. Her eyes moved over to the letter she had written to Thomas a few minutes earlier. It was sitting on the table, sealed and stamped.

At last, a breathless voice answered. "Hello?" Phone calls were rarely happy occasions these days.

"Jeannie, it's Jane," Jane whispered into the receiver.

"Jane! What's happening? Are you okay?"

"I'm okay but I need your help."

"What do you need?"

"Can you get enough gas to come down here?"

"Probably. I get gas coupons to get feed for the cows. But why?"

Jane recounted to Jeannie what had transpired over the last week.

"Seriously? I can't believe you rescued an enemy sailor!" Jane exclaimed through the phone line.

"He isn't an enemy sailor."

"He's a defector then?" asked Jeannie, concern thick in her voice.

"He's an American citizen who jumped ship. We need to help him."

Jane heard a loud huff. "Are you sure about this? Are you sure he is who he says he is? And even if he is, are you sure you should help him under the circumstances?"

"No, I'm not sure about anything. But I *think* it's right."

"Then why are you calling me? What do I need to do?"

"When Doc says he is well, I want you to come get him and take him to my house while I work on another plan. In the meantime, I need you to collect some food for him and get the house set up."

"Get food? In case you haven't heard, we are on a government-ordered rationing program. We barely have enough for ourselves." There was silence on the line for a time. Then Jeannie whispered, "Okay. I'll do what I can."

Two weeks later, as March came in like the proverbial lion, Jeannie pulled up to Jane's cabin in an old farm pickup with wooden sides. Jane and Stephan hustled through the wind and rain to the door of the cab before Jeannie could even get out.

"Nice day for a drive!" Jeannie said with a smile for Stephan.

"I'll say, but it beats beach patrol," he said as he scooted into the middle of the bench seat ahead of Jane.

Jane climbed in the cab and slammed the door shut. Leaning over Stephan she smiled at Jeannie. "Thanks, Jeannie. You are the best friend anyone could ever ask for."

Jeannie snorted. "You mean the stupidest friend, don't you?" She turned to Stephan. "What do you think of John's idea?"

"He knows."

Jeannie raised an eyebrow and cocked her head.

Stephan smiled. "Yep. I know all about Jane."

A look of shock crossed over Jeannie's face. She took a deep breath. "Well, that's an interesting development."

Jane and Stephan laughed.

"Well, what do you think about *Jane's* idea?" Jeannie said, rephrasing her question.

"As I've gotten to know Brian, I believe his story and I'm convinced we should help him."

Jeannie pursed her lips and nodded. "Okay, then. Where's the patient?"

Jane pointed ahead. "Just down the road."

28

March 1943

Jeannie, Stephan, and Jane pulled up in front of the Dirksen home. Jane saw the window curtains part briefly then return to their closed position. The front door opened, and Melanie came out on the porch, struggling to open an umbrella.

Jane and Stephan jumped out of the truck and ran through the rain to the front porch.

"Good morning, Mrs. Dirksen," Stephan said. "Let me help you with that." He took the umbrella from her and pushed the center up. Holding the curved handle tightly, he held it over her head.

"Thank you, young man," she said. Motioning to an old leather satchel on the porch, she added, "Doc and I put together some things for Brian." She smiled at Jane. "He came empty-handed, you know."

Jane hugged Melanie. "Thank you for all you have done for him," she whispered in her ear.

"Oh, young man, it was a pleasure. I don't think we have ever had a more polite guest. My only hope is that we will see him again one day."

Jane grabbed the satchel and carried it out to the pickup. She hoisted it over the wooden sides and covered the bag with a canvas tarp to protect it from the rain. By the time she turned around, Doc was helping Brian down the steps. Stephan followed behind, protecting them with the umbrella.

Jane was pleased to see that Brian was moving quite well. Several weeks under Doc's care had proven to be beneficial.

"You're a miracle worker," Jane said to Doc.

"Naw. I had a great patient."

Before getting in the truck, Brian turned and threw his arms around Doc. Jane felt her throat constrict and tears sting her eyes.

"Now, you get in that truck. I don't want you catching your death of cold," Doc said.

Pulling back, Brian waved at Melanie. "Thank you, Mrs. Dirksen."

"It was a pleasure," she said, smiling broadly. "Now don't be a stranger."

"I won't. I'll be back as soon as I can." Brian climbed into the truck. Jane shut the door. The sailor rolled down the window and Jane said. "Remember the plan."

Brian nodded.

"I'll get a hold of you as soon as I know something."

"John, I can't thank you enough. Someday I'll repay you. I'll repay all of you."

"You just take care of yourself . . . oh, and don't burn down my house!"

"I'll do my best," he said with a smile. He rolled the window up. Jeannie stepped on the clutch and shifted into first gear.

Jane, Stephan, and Doc stood huddled under the umbrella and watched them pull away.

When the truck was out of sight, Doc turned to Jane. "So, what's next?"

Jane shrugged her shoulders. "I don't know for sure. I'm waiting to get a letter back from my friend Thomas Kato."

For the next week, Jane ran to the mailbox every day hoping for a response to her letter. At the end of the month, the much-anticipated letter finally arrived. She tore open the letter before she even reached the front porch.

March 15, 1943

Dear Jane,

I am sorry to be so slow responding to your inquiry. At first, I was very confused by your letter. You are a Sand Pounder? How can that be? The Sand Pounders are all men. I guess you have some stories to tell me if we ever meet again!

You wanted to know if there was a family here by the name of Kikomoto from Placerville, California. Since there are now over 15,000 Japanese here, it took me quite a while to get an answer. In fact, if it weren't for my father's connections with the Caucasian family that is in charge of the camp, it would have taken much longer. You see, we are divided into groups based upon our living quarters and we never really get to mingle with the other groups. The only time we do is when a baseball team from one barracks plays another. But you don't need to know about that. The answer to your question is "YES!" There is a family here by the name of Kikomoto. I was able to track them down when my father told me which barracks they are in. I showed them your letter and both the parents cried for joy. They had feared the worst when they heard their son had been forced to join the Japanese Navy. They had not heard a word from him since that happened.

They are eagerly awaiting more news and pray that their son has recovered from his injuries. I assured them that you could be trusted to do the right thing by their son.

I'm very interested to hear more about all of this.

Your Friend,
Thomas

29

April 1943

A few days after Jane received the letter from Thomas, the Coast Guard Commander arrived at the house where the four Lincoln City Sand Pounders were based. Jane and Stephan were in the corral, feeding the horses and mucking the pen. Jane looked up, surprised to see the Commander standing outside the fence.

Perspiration arose on Jane's forehead and her heart started pounding. She wiped her forehead with her sleeve and set the manure fork against the side of the barn. *Does he know about Brian?* she thought. "Commander," she said, forcing a smile. "To what do we owe the honor of a visit." Hearing Jane speaking, Stephan spun around. He watched as Jane walked up to the fence, then joined her.

The Commander smiled, easing Jane's anxiety a bit. "Hello, Coast Guardsmen Morris and Peters." He looked around. "I trust Coast Guardsmen Tindal and Armstrong are out on patrol."

"They are, sir," Stephan said.

"I have come to make a change in your assignment."

Jane raised her eyebrows.

"We have some new recruits that are just finishing their training. Since the four of you are now experienced, I would like to move you to a different part of the sector. I'd like to keep the new Sand Pounders closer to the post."

Jane felt her shoulders sag with relief. Her breathing slowed and she smiled at Stephan. Stephan smiled back and Jane was sure he had been feeling the same anxiety she had.

Stephan looked back at the Commander. "We are here to serve. Send us wherever you need us."

"I need you on the Oregon-California border. You'll be stationed at Brookings."

"Excuse me, sir," Jane said. "Are you sending all four of us?"

"Just the two of you will go to Brookings. I'm sending Tindal and Armstrong to Washington."

The Commander gave them their travel instructions. "A truck and trailer will be available for you on Friday, two weeks from today at 1100 hours. I can't spare the men to drive you down, so you'll have to go by yourselves. We have arranged for you to stay with a local family. I trust you are both perfectly capable of driving a horse trailer," he added with a chuckle.

As soon as the Commander drove away, Jane threw her arms around Stephan. "I can't believe this!" she squealed, letting go of her man voice.

Stephan blushed. "Can't believe what?" he said, returning the hug.

"This is the answer to my prayers!"

"How so?"

"Don't you see? This is how we can get Brian down to Tule Lake to be reunited with his family!"

Jane ran into the house to pen a letter to Thomas.

April 4, 1943

Dear Thomas,

I have exciting news. My partner and I are being transferred from Lincoln City to Brookings. We will leave here with our horses on Friday, April 16th. You told me your father had access to a car. I am hoping he can meet us in Klamath Falls on Saturday morning. We will have Brian Kikomoto with us. You can call Dr. Dirksen at Neptune 6-6272 and tell us where to meet and what time. Doc can be trusted.

Oh . . . one more thing. He thinks my name is John.
Your friend,
Jane

Now Jane's only worry was if the letter would arrive on time.

Dennis Dirksen was surprised by the ringing of the telephone early Monday morning, April 12th.

"Dr. Dirksen?"

"Yes, this is he."

"My name is Mr. Kato. I am an old friend of Ja . . . uhmmm . . . John Morris."

"Oh, yes. John the Sand Pounder," Doc responded.

"I have been asked to call you to confirm a meeting time and place with John on Saturday, April 17th. She . . . *he* has asked me to pick up a delivery."

"You needn't worry. I know all about Brian Kikomoto. You can give me the message and I will see that *John* gets it," Doc said, a twinkle in his eye.

"Thank you, very much. Tell *him* to meet me at the Safeway in Klamath Falls at noon on Saturday. If there should be any difficulty and one or the other of us misses the rendezvous, have him leave Brian at Monty's Motel and I will find him there."

"That I will do," Doc said.

That evening, as Jane and Stephan were tacking up to begin their patrol, Doc approached the corral.

"Hello, Sand Pounders," he called out.

Jane and Stephan turned from where they stood cinching up their girths. "Hey, Doc," Stephan called out.

"I have some news for *John*," he said with a chuckle.

Jane led her horse to the gate. "What is it? Have you heard from Thomas?"

"I believe it was his father. He identified himself as Mr. Kato."

Jane smiled. "Yes. That would be him. He's very formal."

"That's alright with me. I like that in a man," Doc said.

"What did he say?" Jane said, feeling a slight tremble course up her spine.

"It's all set," Doc said. He proceeded to give an account of the phone conversation.

When Doc finished, he took Jane's hand and looked her in the eyes. "Have you been keeping something from me, young *lady*?"

Jane blushed and dropped her chin to her chest. Stephan stood to one side and grinned.

"Don't worry. I won't tell anyone," Doc said, giving her hand a squeeze. "Your secret is safe with me."

Once Dr. Dirksen left, the Sand Pounders mounted up and headed for the beach. They passed Tim and Chip who were finished with their patrol and heading home. Once out of earshot of their friends, Jane turned back in the saddle and grinned at Stephan. "We can do this. We can get Brian back to his family."

"I hope so," Stephan said. "It's amazing that things appear to be working out so smoothly. How do you suppose Doc figured out you're a girl?"

Jane shook her head. "I don't know. I thought I was faking it pretty well. Maybe Mr. Kato let it slip. But I'm not worried about Doc. He'll keep my secret . . . he said he would."

They rode on in silence for a few minutes.

"I do have one last worry," Jane finally said, breaking the silence between them.

"What's that?"

"How will Mr. Kato get Brian into the camp?"

Stephan shook his head. "I don't know, but my guess is there aren't too many people trying to sneak *in* the camp so maybe the guards at the gate aren't very vigilant when cars come in."

Jane nodded as she stroked Star's neck. "I'll bet you're right."

30

April 1943

As soon as Jane returned from patrol the next morning, she dismounted and handed her reins to Stephan. "Would you mind untacking and feeding? I'm eager to call Brian."

"I'll bet you are," Stephan said. "Sure. I'll take care of the horses," he added, giving Jane a quick hug.

Jane nearly skipped to the house, too excited from both Stephan's hug and the upcoming call to feel tired.

She used her finger on the rotary dial to call the phone at her home, a number her family had always used. As she listened to the phone ring, she heard the familiar click of someone else on the party line picking up. Her heart leaped to her throat and she slammed the receiver down.

Jane paced around the room, watching the second hand move slowly around the face of the round wall clock over the kitchen sink. *How long will they talk?* she wondered. As she waited, she opened a can of SPAM and sliced it. Pulling out a frying pan, she placed the slices in the pan and started heating them up for herself and Stephan. She added a couple of eggs to fry and waited, tapping the spatula on the side of the pan. Her eyes darted back and forth between the clock and the phone. Deciding she couldn't wait any longer, she pulled the pan off the burner and went to the phone. Covering the mouthpiece, she quietly lifted the receiver off the cradle and placed it to her ear.

She heard a woman, whose voice she recognized as being a long-time member of her party line, chattering away. "I know if I came across one of those *evil Japs*, I'd turn them in immediately."

Jane's breath caught in her throat. She gently but hurriedly placed the receiver back in the cradle. She sat down at the table, folded her arms on top, and dropped her head. *What have I done? What if someone finds Brian?*

When Stephan returned from caring for the horses, he found Jane asleep at the table and the smell of SPAM filling the kitchen. Stephan had a delightful breakfast watching Jane sleep.

After finishing his breakfast, Stephan stepped over to where Jane sat sleeping and shook her shoulder. "Wake up, sleepyhead. Move into your bunk so you can get a good day's rest." This was his daily joke when they were on the night shift.

Jane jerked awake. Her eyes opened wide, and her hands flew to her cheeks. "How long was I asleep?"

"Not long."

Pushing back her chair she ran to the phone. "I have to call Brian," she said as she picked up the receiver. Hearing nothing but the dial tone, she knew no one else was on the line. She dialed her home phone, hoping Brian would pick up quickly before anyone else tried to join in.

To Jane, it seemed Friday would never arrive. There would be no time for sleeping that day. Once they completed their patrol, they would need to take care of the horses then pack all their gear. Jane was expecting Jeannie to arrive by nine in the morning after picking up Brian an hour earlier.

When nine arrived, Jeannie did not. Jane paced the kitchen floor, watching the clock then peeking out the window, back to the clock, then back to the window. With each revolution of the second hand, Jane's anxiety grew.

"It's okay, Jane," Stephan said, trying to offer comfort. "Jeannie probably got tied up at the dairy farm."

Jane pressed her lips tightly together and nodded. But her pacing continued.

At 9:30, Jane heard the crunch of tires on the gravel drive. She ran to the door and threw it open. A sigh of relief left her lips as she spotted Jeannie behind the wheel of the truck. She ran out the door.

"I've been so worried about you. Is everything okay?"

"No. We nearly got caught by the Olsons!" Jeannie said as she and Brian climbed out of the truck.

"What do you mean?" Jane asked.

"They saw me drive up to your house and came over to talk. Thankfully, Brian saw them and stayed in the house until they were gone."

"What did they say?"

"They wanted to know where you and Star were. I didn't know what to tell them, so I made up a big lie about you working on a ranch in Montana!"

Jane laughed. "Montana, huh? Thanks for covering for me." She turned her attention to Brian. "Brian, leave your bag on the porch then go down to the Dirksen's house. Doc and Mrs. Dirksen want a visit," she said with a smile.

"It'll be my pleasure."

"And stay there until we come to get you," she called to his back as he headed to the porch with his bag. "We want to make sure the Coast Guardsman that brings the trailer is long gone." He waved a hand in acknowledgement.

Jane and Jeannie went in the house, Jane to finish packing and Jeannie to flirt with Stephan.

At 1100 hours on the dot, an army truck pulling a two-horse trailer arrived. It was followed by another truck. Inside the trailer were two horses, stomping and whinnying. The new Sand Pounders, who were to replace Jane and Stephan, jumped out of the truck and unloaded their horses.

Jane and Stephan brought Star and Big Bay to the trailer and loaded them up. They helped the newcomers get settled before loading their own gear in the back of the truck. By 1120 hours Stephan and Jane left their Lincoln City home, picked up Brian, and headed down Highway 101.

31

April 1943

In 1942 the Federal Government instituted a nationwide 35-mile-per-hour speed limit. The intent was to reduce wear on tires as rubber was fast becoming a scarce commodity. The curving coastal highway that Stephan was driving made pulling a horse trailer any faster impossible anyway. The 230-mile drive took more than seven hours, including two stops for gas at coastal towns along the way. Fortunately, the Commander had left gas coupons in an envelope on the dashboard. Whenever they stopped, they hid Brian under a blanket in the back of the cab so no one would see him and report them.

As they approached Brookings, they passed one of the several bulb farms that had started making the town famous before the war broke out. In 1940 Brookings had started producing

Easter lily bulbs, and the farmers hoped to make it the biggest producer of bulbs in North America. That remained to be seen; at this time, no one was famous for anything except war-related businesses.

The Sand Pounders and their horses pulled into the little town of Brookings at seven at night, or 1900 hours as the Commander would say. As they drove through the tiny main street that ran along the Coastal Highway, they noticed that most of the stores were closed and darkened, ready for the early curfews the coastal towns obeyed. At last, they found a gas station. The garage doors that signaled the entrance to the repair shop were still open and they could see someone moving around inside. They stopped to get directions to the address of the home where they were staying.

"Ah, that's the Widow Mullin's place," the store owner said. "She is just over the Chetco River in the town of Harbor. Third road on your right after you've crossed the bridge. If you get to California, you've gone five miles too far south."

He paused and looked them over more carefully. "Coast Guard? You from the station up in Florence?"

"Tillamook Bay," Stephan said.

"What're you doin' way down here?" he asked. The look on his face indicated he was more curious than suspicious.

"We're Sand Pounders. We have come to patrol the beaches."

"Well, I'm mighty glad to hear that. None of us have gotten over worrying about an invasion since the Japs tried to burn us out with them crazy balloon contraptions."

Jane and Stephan thanked the station owner for his help and climbed back in the truck. Once they were driving on the road, Brian sat up. "Whew. It was getting hot under these blankets," he said using the blanket to wipe his forehead.

"I hear Brookings is called the Banana Belt of the Oregon Coast," Jane said.

Stephan rolled his eyes. "I don't think I'd go that far."

"No, really. The winds come from the east through the Klamath Mountains, right down the Chetco River. They blow the marine layer, you know, the fog and clouds that sit over the ocean, out to sea. They have more sunshine down here than the other places on the coast."

Stephan took his eyes off the road long enough to look over at Jane, his brows raised. "So, *John,* when we are done saving the world are you going to become a weatherman?"

Jane turned her head and looked forward with a smile on her face. "I just might . . . if I don't make it to the Olympics on Star . . . if there ever will be an Olympics again."

The sun was setting, sending an orange streak across the sea from the horizon to the shore, when they pulled into the drive running up to Mrs. Mullin's house. Stopping beside the house, Jane climbed down from the truck and went to the door. The house was weather-beaten, the paint around the windows and on the door was peeling. But Easter lilies were growing in the well-tended garden that lined the path to the door.

Jane stepped up to the door and knocked. As she waited, she heard a high-pitched bark from a dog and the sound of shuffling steps. The door opened.

"Well, I declare, I didn't think you'd ever get here," said a short, plump woman with gray hair and pale blue eyes. "I've been trying to keep dinner warm for an hour."

"Mrs. Mullin?" Jane said with a smile and outstretched hand. "I'm John Morris from the Coast Guard Sand Pounders."

Mrs. Mullin took her hand. Jane noticed how boney and cold the woman's hand was; she couldn't stop herself from covering it with both her hands.

Mrs. Mullin smiled. "Figured as much . . . though I must say you're too pretty to be a boy. Shame to waste those eye lashes on a boy," she added with a chuckle.

Jane felt her cheeks redden, as she lowered her eyelids. "I appreciate the dinner, but could we take care of the horses first?"

"Oh course, young man. Just drive your truck down the lane. You'll see the barn and paddock. I had some hay and grain delivered yesterday. I hope you find it satisfactory. Some horse people can be awfully picky."

"I'm sure our horses will love it. Thank you."

The barn and paddock at the back of the Mullin property, while long deserted, was in good repair. Though grayed with the weather, even the wooden fences seemed to be holding up well.

Stephan and Brian went into the barn to check out the living quarters for both man and equine. Jane went to the back of the trailer and unlatched one of the half doors and the butt-bar that clipped from the side to the center divider. "Step back, Star, step back." Star shuffled her hooves, feeling for the end of the trailer and the resulting drop. Lowering one hoof at a time she backed out of the straight-load trailer. Big Bay craned his neck and watched her go. Irritated that he had been left behind, he began stomping and pawing.

Once out of the trailer, Jane clipped a lead rope to the mare's halter as the horse looked around. Her nostrils flared, sucking in the strange smells. Her ears twitched first one way then another, picking up strange sounds caused by the wind curling through the bent trees. Her eyes widened, searching the unfamiliar surroundings.

"It's okay, girl. This is our new home. At least for a while." She led her to the paddock gate and let her go inside. The mare lifted her head and trotted around the fence line of the small enclosure. Meanwhile, Big Bay let his irritation at being left alone be known with loud whinnies and kicks at the sides of the trailer.

"I'm coming, Big Bay. Settle down," Jane said as she opened the other side of the back door. Big Bay started backing out before the butt bar was unhooked, one leg slipping off the back of the trailer.

"No!" Jane said, panic in her voice. "Get up there," she said slapping him on the rump. The horse brought his leg up and stepped forward enough for Jane to unhook the bar. Big Bay backed out quickly and ran over to the paddock before Jane could attach the lead rope. He trotted up and down the fence beside Star. Jane stopped and placed her hands on her hips in frustration.

"Stephan! Stephan!" she shouted toward the barn. "Come get your horse!"

Stephan came at a run from the barn. He grabbed the lead rope from Jane as he passed by her. Slowing to a walk he coaxed Big Bay. "Hey, big boy, what kind of tomfoolery are you up to?" The horse stopped and turned to face him. He let out a loud snort but didn't move.

Stephan walked up to him and clipped the lead rope to his halter. Turning to Jane he said, "Bring Star in the barn. We have their stalls ready."

Jane led Star from the paddock and followed behind Big Bay. She bit her lip and squinted her eyes as she watched Big Bay walking. Clearly, he was limping on a hind leg. "Stephan, stop," she called out.

Stephan stopped and turned back toward Jane. "What is it?"

"Check his near hind," she said as she caught up.

Sure enough, the leg Big Bay had dropped out of the trailer was bleeding. Stephan looked up at Jane, his eyes questioning.

"He did that when he backed out of the trailer."

Stephan crouched down beside the injured leg. He sighed and shook his head. "Well, it happens. Let's find the ointment and bandages."

As Brian watched, the two Sand Pounders soon had Big Bay doctored up. "I'm impressed," he said when they were done. "No wonder I'm still alive."

"Your injuries were a lot more serious," Jane said, patting him on the shoulder. "Now, we need to get to the house. Mrs. Mullin has waited way too long for dinner. We'll bring you something."

"If there's anything left!" Stephan said, giving Brian a punch in the arm.

32

April 1943

After a lovely and filling dinner, Stephan and Jane returned to the barn. Their stomachs had not been treated with such fine cooking since they had joined the Coast Guard. It reminded Jane of meals with her grandmother and aunt. She felt an ache in her heart and resolved to write a letter to them immediately.

"Did you bring me anything?" Brian said hopefully as the Sand Pounders entered the back room of the barn.

Jane pulled a chunk of bread and cheese from her jacket pocket.

Stephan produced a piece of apple pie.

"How did you get this?" Brian said, his eyes wide with excitement at the sight of the pie.

"I told her I wanted to save it for a midnight snack."

"You're the best!" Brian said, grabbing the plate and fork.

"You really should eat your dinner first," Jane teased.

"Yes, Dad," Brian said, taking the bread and cheese. Stephan winked at Jane.

"Let's get to bed," Stephan said. "We have a long drive tomorrow, and Mr. Kato is expecting us at noon. I suggest we leave by six in the morning."

The Sand Pounders made themselves comfortable in the tack room where two cots had been set up. Brian snuck to the pickup and slept across the bench seat with a blanket covering him.

Before the sun had risen over the Klamath Mountains, the horses had been fed, Big Bay's bandage changed, the trailer unhooked, and the three were off in the pickup. They drove south for several miles, crossing into California, before turning northeast on Highway 197 then left again on 199 that took them back into Oregon.

Without the gas coupons Jeannie had snuck to them, they wouldn't be making this trip at all.

The five-hour drive took them first through Grants Pass, then to Medford, and finally east to Klamath Falls. Jane was quiet most of the trip, enjoying the beauty around them as they climbed one mountain pass after another. Yet there was an undeniable knot in her stomach. Clearly, what they were doing was breaking the law by harboring a Japanese boy, even if he was an American citizen. Beyond that, there still remained so many variables. What if Mr. Kato couldn't get to Klamath Falls by noon? Or even at all? Would the people at the motel that they were using for a backup plan report a Japanese man on their premises? And *if* Mr. Kato met them, would he be able to get Brian into the camp and reunited with his family? Sometimes she thought she must be crazy to even try this . . . and now was one of those times.

On occasion, Jane caught Stephan driving faster than the required thirty-five miles an hour, but she didn't say anything. She was grateful he was willing to risk delivering Brian to meet Mr. Kato.

She pulled her eyes off the speedometer and looked back out the window. Jane had never been this far south or east in Oregon and she was surprised at how barren it was as they drove from Medford to Klamath Falls. Growing up on the Oregon Coast, she naturally assumed the entire state was covered with dripping evergreens and gray clouds. Not so in Klamath Falls. The farther they drove from Medford, the drier and hotter it became. Fields planted with potatoes and cattle grazing on dry grass in wire-fenced pastures lined the road. At an isolated road-side café, Stephan and Jane stopped to get sodas to cool off, bringing one back to the car for Brian.

As they approached Klamath Falls, not only did several buildings and homes come into view, but they noticed numerous Navy planes approaching and landing, and others taking off.

In 1928, the citizens of Klamath Falls constructed an airport. They named it Klamath Falls Municipal Airport. Its runways were nothing more than long, gravel strips . . . but it worked. In 1942, at the start of the war, the airport was selected as a site for a Naval Air Station. It was just far enough from the Pacific to keep it safe, yet close enough to make it convenient. The entire airport was transferred to the U.S. Navy. This brought new business into the town as Navy aviators and sailors spent their free time at the restaurants and taverns that lined the downtown and outlying areas.

Stephan drove the truck into town. Few people paid any attention to the green Army truck. While Stephan kept his eyes on the road, Jane and Brian watched out the windows for a Safeway grocery store. Just five minutes before the set rendezvous time of noon, they spotted the store's large sign ahead.

"There it is," Brian said, pointing.

"I see it," Stephan responded.

"Wait!" cried out Jane. "That's Mr. Kato across the street. What's going on?"

On the opposite street corner, a group of men in Naval Air Command uniforms were surrounding Mr. Kato. Some of the men were pushing him as others raised their voices.

Stephan pulled the pickup into a parking spot just down the street. "Hide!" he commanded Brian as he jumped out of the truck.

"I'm coming, too," Jane said as she bounded out the passenger door and slammed it shut behind her.

The two Coast Guardsmen jogged down the sidewalk toward the crowd gathering around Mr. Kato.

"Hey! What's going on?" Stephan said, pushing a sailor aside and stepping into the center of the crowd. Jane followed in his wake.

One tall sailor turned, a sneer still on his face which softened as he sized up Stephan. "A Coast Guardsman? Aren't you a bit out of your territory?"

Stephan ignored the jibe. "I said, 'What's going on?' Are you going to tell me or not?"

Jane squeezed in beside Stephan. She looked at Mr. Kato. The slight smile on his face told her he recognized her.

"Well, you've got eyes," the Navy man said. "This here's a dirty Jap. I want to know why he's out of his cell."

Stephan lifted his chin. "Did you ask him?"

"Why should I? It's plain enough he's not where he belongs."

The crowd around them responded with "Yeah," and "That's right!" and "Send him to the camps." A few fists shook in the air.

Jane looked from side to side. For all her worrying about what could go wrong, she hadn't considered this. Her face turned pallid, and her limbs began to shake. She wanted to grab Mr. Kato and run. She looked up at Stephan and saw the anger building in him as his face reddened and the muscles of his jaw twitched.

With teeth clenched, Stephan said, "I say we ask him."

"Be my guest," said the sailor with a sweep of his arm.

Lowering his voice, Stephan turned to Mr. Kato. His tone softened. "Sir, where do you live?"

"I'm from Tillamook but am currently a resident of the Tule Lake Internment Camp."

"Yeah! Ask him why he's not there now!" someone in the crowd shouted.

Mr. Kato looked over the crowd toward the speaker. "I am the camp chef for the Caucasian families who are in charge. Every few weeks, I come to Klamath Falls to buy groceries. I was heading to the store, minding my own business, when these men stopped me."

"Proof!" yelled the lead antagonist. "I'd like to see some proof, wouldn't you?" he shouted to the crowd.

Shouts of agreement filtered through the group.

"I have papers right here," Mr. Kato said as he rifled through his breast pocket. Pulling one out, he shook it in the air. "See. It's right here." He handed it to Stephan.

Stephan scanned it, then turned and faced the crowd. "This is a letter from the camp commander giving Mr. Kato permission to use the camp car to acquire needed groceries. Everything he said is true. Now I suggest you all go about your business and let this man do his."

With some grumbling, the mob dispersed. Some looked shamefaced, but others still seemed resistant and angry.

"Thank you," Mr. Kato said when everyone was gone.

"Glad we were here," Jane said.

"As am I. But it is too dangerous to carry out our exchange here. Go to plan B at one this afternoon." Mr. Kato walked across the street and entered the Safeway store.

33

April 1943

An hour later, Stephan parked the truck outside Monty's Motel. The lodging was located on the outskirts of town on the road that went to Crater Lake, the only national park in Oregon. A new green and white sign posted along the road that read "Monty's Motel," beckoned travelers. Below the name, in bold lettering was painted: "Crater Later-Rest Here First."

Motels were a fairly new idea, born as more Americans traveled the U.S. by car, and Jane was sure it had plenty of business in peacetime. At this time, there were no cars parked in front of any of the buildings. The motel itself was set back a bit from the road and consisted of a large, green, clapboard structure with white trim along the roofline and around the windows. All of this was accented with a bright red door. This housed the office and a home for the owner. Beyond this building was a row of small cabin-like buildings for guests, painted in the same welcoming green and white. The grounds in front were covered with high desert plants and lava rocks. Pride of ownership was clearly evident.

Jane, Stephan, and Brian sat in the truck, staring at the building and trying to decide their next move. "Mr. Kato's first message said to leave Brian here," said Jane in a whisper. "But, after what happened this morning, I'm afraid to."

"My concern is also for the horses," Stephan said. "They will need feeding in a few hours. What will Mrs. Mullin think if we don't return to take care of them?"

"We told her we would be gone all day on a Coast Guard assignment," Jane responded.

"Yes, but we also told her we'd be back in time to take care of the horses." Stephan removed his cap and combed his fingers through his hair.

"If Mr. Kato said to leave me here, he must know and trust the owner," Brian said.

Jane chewed on her thumb nail and kept her eyes glued to the office door.

All sat in silence until the door opened and a tall, thin man emerged and walked directly to their truck. Jane noticed the hint of gray in his hair and guessed him to be old enough to be her father. He wore a plaid shirt tucked into green twill slacks. He had a stony expression on his face that

Jane could not read. Three pairs of eyes followed him as he approached the driver's side of the pickup and tapped on the window. Stephan rolled it down.

"You friends of Mr. Kato's?" he asked as the corners of his mouth turned up.

Jane said little on the drive home. Her sense of relief was mixed with continuing concern for Brian. Mr. Kato still needed to pick him up and get him into the camp. She wished she'd had a chance to talk to Mr. Kato instead of just leaving Brian at Monty's Motel. She sighed.

"You okay?" Stephan said, reaching over and patting her arm.

Jane smiled at him. "I sure appreciate you."

"Oh, fiddlesticks," he said. "I didn't do anything you wouldn't have done." But the smile on his face showed he was pleased.

The next day, Jane and Stephan began their patrol of the beaches on both sides of the harbor.

With only two Sand Pounders patrolling this stretch of the coastline, Jane and Stephan were assigned to cover the night duty. Dog patrols were covering the daytime hours.

Night patrol was pleasant enough with the warmer weather arriving in the Banana Belt of the Oregon Coast. Jane was learning that the nickname was well deserved. The nights with a full moon would have been, under different circumstances, downright romantic. But night after night and week after week, riding up and down the same coastline became tedious and boring.

The beaches and surf around Brookings were lined with large rocks and were home to a myriad of birds. During high tide, the Sand Pounders often found themselves riding through wild waves with strong undertows as they skirted around rocky outcroppings. On more than one occasion over the next two months, the Sand Pounders came upon a local fisherman whose boat had washed against the rocks. Their state-of-the-art radios were used to call for help. Before long, a Coast Guard boat would arrive to pull the craft safely away from the shore to deeper water.

But that was about the extent of the excitement until the night Big Bay came galloping down the beach without a rider.

34

June 1943

It was a windy night, and the waves were responding with more than their usual gusto. Stephan had taken the lead. Jane was behind him about a quarter of a mile. She rolled her shoulders, trying to adjust the thirty-five-pound radio on her back to a more comfortable position. She didn't mind taking a turn carrying the pack, but that didn't make it any less uncomfortable.

Jane was using her binoculars to scan the horizon where the sea and the sky mingle together. Suddenly, Star snorted and came to a stop, her head up, her ears pricked forward. Jane trained her binoculars into the darkness ahead of them. Then her mouth fell open and she dropped the field glasses to her chest. Galloping toward her was Big Bay . . . riderless. Star, sensing that something was amiss, started prancing around in a circle. Big Bay called out to them with a loud whinny and Star answered in kind. When

Stephan's horse reached them, he came to an abrupt halt, skidding on the wet sand.

Jane reached out and grabbed Big Bay's reins. It was obvious something was wrong. Digging her heels into Star's side, she started galloping down the beach, ponying Big Bay beside her.

When she got to the edge of a rocky outcropping that jutted out into the waves, she saw a dark body against the rock. She knew right away it was Stephan. She dismounted and pulled the heavy radio off her back, setting it on the dry sand. She held onto Big Bay's reins and started leading him toward the ocean. With the horse behind her, she waded into the water. The waves rolled in up to her waist. Big Bay pulled back. "Come on, boy. We need to get to Stephan." Big Bay hesitated. "Come on, I said." She tugged on the reins. When a wave crawled back to sea, Big Bay stepped forward and Jane was able to reach Stephan. He was clinging to the jagged edge of a rock. His eyes were closed. Blood was streaming down his face from a nasty gash on his forehead. But he was alive.

Jane wrapped his arm over her shoulder, dragged him to the sand, and dropped him with an unceremonial thud. She pulled the First Aid kit from Stephan's saddle bag and wrapped a gauze bandage around his head. Having stopped the bleeding, she used the radio to call for help. Then she sat beside Stephan, placed his head on her lap, and waited. It was at that moment, surrounded by the crashing waves and the howling wind, that the infatuation she'd had for Stephan since the day they met became love and she started praying.

A Coast Guard boat from the Port of Brookings answered the call. Jane watched it arrive, following its lights with her binoculars. She signaled them with a flare gun. The boat turned and scooted across the waves toward them. The boat beached nearby but far enough away to avoid crashing into the rocks.

Two Coast Guardsmen leaped from the boat, one carrying a stretcher. They ran up the beach. "What are his vitals?" one man shouted as they approached.

"He's breathing," Jane said. "His heart rate is fine. He just took a bad hit to the head and he's unconscious."

"We'll take it from here," the other man said as they placed Stephan's body on the stretcher.

Jane stood, holding the reins of both horses as she watched them carry Stephan away, place him in the boat, and race back over the tops of the waves. She watched until they were out of sight. Then she let the tears she'd been holding back have their way.

Later that morning, Mrs. Mullin and Jane drove into Brookings to the little hospital in the center of town.

"We're here to check on Stephan Peters," Mrs. Mullin told the receptionist behind the front desk.

"Of course," she said with a kindly smile. "I'll see if he can have visitors."

Jane felt her heart pounding and she tried to slow her breathing to keep calm. Mrs. Mullin put her arm around her shoulders. "There, there, John. Everything will be alright. You'll see. Your partner will be as good as new in no time."

Jane forced a smile and nodded.

A few minutes later, the receptionist returned. "Follow me, please," she said, turning and walking ahead of them down the short hallway. She stopped at a door and motioned for them to go inside. "Please don't be long. We don't want to wear him out."

Jane quietly entered the darkened room.

"Hey John! Come in," Stephan said, his voice sounding strong and cheerful.

Jane stepped up to the side of the bed. Mrs. Mullin followed behind.

"Can you fluff up these pillows?" he asked.

"Sure," Jane said as she propped the pillows against his back.

A smile spread across his face. "I like having you wait on me."

"Don't get used to it," Jane said. A flood of relief coursed through her. This was Stephan. He was going to be okay.

"Hi, Mrs. Mullin," Stephan said, turning his attention to their hostess. "So nice of you to come."

"I just wanted to see how long I needed to cut my meals in half. You eat enough for the both of us, you know," she said with a wink of her eye.

"Not long. I'll be out of here soon. Doc says I'm nearly as healthy as my horse." He turned his attention back to Jane. "Thanks for rescuing me," he said, his eyes warm. "How'd you know I was there?"

"Big Bay came galloping down the beach without you. It didn't take much for me to figure out that something was wrong. What happened?"

"We were trying to ride around that rock when an enormous wave came upon us. I tried to turn and get to shore before it hit, but I didn't make it. It went right over us and pushed me off my saddle. Last thing I remember, I was being tossed around in the water like a piece of driftwood. The next thing I knew, I was in here."

Jane turned to Mrs. Mullin. "Would you mind getting us something to drink? A cola, perhaps?"

"Be glad to," she said as she went out the door.

Jane turned back to Stephan. In her natural voice she said, "Stephan, I was so scared."

He took her hand and squeezed it. "You saved my life, just like Brian. Now you have two men who owe their lives to you."

"It was different this time," she said, looking away. She took a deep breath then in a whisper she said, "I . . . I don't know what I'd do if I lost you."

"Jane."

Jane turned back and looked into his eyes.

"Jane, I've been in love with you ever since I figured out your secret."

Jane leaned forward; her eyes closed. But before their lips could meet, she heard . . .

"I knew it!" Jane's eyes popped open and she turned to see Mrs. Mullin in the doorway, holding two bottles of Dr. Pepper. "I knew you were a girl the minute I laid eyes on you. 'Balderdash,' I told myself, 'That's a girl if I ever done seen one.'"

Jane and Stephan looked at each other then broke out in laughter.

Stephan reached up and pulled Jane down. Their first kiss was mirific.

35

June 1943

The next day, the Commander arrived at the hospital to visit his Sand Pounder. Stephan saw him enter the room and sat up in bed. Jane turned and, seeing the Commander, stood at attention.

"At ease, Sand Pounders."

"Commander, thank you for coming," Stephan said.

"I heard you were injured in the line of duty," the Commander said. "You can't trust those dangerous waves," he said with a twinkle in his eye.

"Yes, sir," Stephan said.

Turning to Jane he said, "It appears you handled things perfectly, young man."

"Thank you, sir," she said.

"Coast Guardsman Peters, what is the prognosis?"

"Oh, sir, I'll be fine as soon as my head wound is healed."

"Do you plan to return to duty?"

"Of course, sir. I'll be back on my horse in a day or two."

"Good. Good," he said nodding his head and smiling. "In the meantime," he said, turning back to Jane, "I'll have you, Coast Guardsman Morris, patrol with the K-9 unit. It is against regulations for you to patrol on horseback alone."

"Yes, sir," Jane responded.

Turning back to Stephan, he said, "Now, get back to the job of healing and let me know when you are ready to return to duty."

"I will, sir. Thank you," said Stephan.

In some locations, the Coast Guard used both horses and dogs in its patrol. Dogs were more frequently used along beaches where the access was difficult for a horse. Both the Sand Pounders and the K-9 unit were sent to Brookings as a result of the attempted fire-bombing.

Jane and Stephan had minimal contact with the two Coast Guardsmen and the dogs in the time they had been in Brookings. Both sets of partners had been busy with their own duties and were not housed close together. But Jane was not concerned. In fact, she was eager to get to work with them, if even for just a few days. Star was not a big fan of large dogs, but these dogs were highly trained, and Jane felt comfortable that the men could control them.

Jane met the K-9 unit by the Harbor the very next morning. "Coast Guardsmen Smith and Wells, I presume?" she said as she rode up to them. Star stopped a few yards back, but the dogs stayed seated beside their handlers, poised and alert.

"That's us," said the shortest of the two. He smiled broadly. "I'm Guardsman Smith. You're Guardsman Morris, no doubt. We're happy to work with you."

"Thank you," Jane said.

"Beautiful horse you have there," said the second man, no doubt Wells.

Jane reached down and stroked Star's neck. "Thank you. Your dogs are magnificent."

The patrol with the K-9 unit was a fun diversion for Jane. Star soon became accustomed to the dogs walking or jogging beside them.

Their responsibilities remained the same and all went well for the three days that Jane joined them.

Returning from patrol at dusk on the third day, Jane was met by Mrs. Mullin at the top of the driveway. "I have good news for you," she said while pulling bobby pins out of the tight curls that covered her head.

"Stephan?" Jane said, standing up in her stirrups.

"The doctors said he can come home. You can pick him up."

36

June 1943

In the two months since she had dropped Brian off in Klamath Falls, Jane had checked the mailbox daily for a letter from either Brian or Thomas. She could not stop worrying about Brian and Mr. Kato and didn't know if the silence was a good sign or a bad sign. The one thing she did know was that waiting was pure torture. As each day passed without word, her impatience increased. She'd slam the mailbox shut and mutter under her breath, "What's taking them so long? Why hasn't one of them written to me? Don't they know how worried I am?"

Couple this with the fact that she had not heard from her brother for more than three months and she had plenty on her mind.

At last, she was rewarded. Letters from both Thomas and Brian arrived in the same envelope.

Jane pulled out both letters and smoothed them out on the leather seat of the saddle she was cleaning. She picked up the letter from Brian first.

May 16, 1943

Dear John or Jane,

My heart is full of gratitude for all you have done for me. It seems a strange thing to thank someone for sending me to "prison," but without you, I would not have been reunited with my family.

Let me fill you in on what has happened since you left me at Monty's Motel. The proprietor is really named Mr. Montgomery. He was an old school buddy of Mr. Kato's when they were in college at Oregon State. He kindly served me a bounteous lunch as we waited. Mr. Kato arrived shortly thereafter. I must say, he was sad to not have the opportunity to visit with you. He certainly likes you. He did tell me that your name is Jane, not John. Someday you must tell me that story!

But, aside from that, the hour-long drive to Tule Lake was uneventful until we approached the gates to the camp. When we arrived, as pure luck would have it, we were right behind a group of Japanese people who were being transferred from a camp in Jerome, Arkansas. That camp is being downsized with the intention of eventually being closed, and the internees are being dispersed to other camps. I later learned that many of the people who had been shipped to Arkansas were originally from California. I have no idea why they would send them so far away in the first place. There are other, much closer, camps. It is surprising, however, that they would bring them here as the camp population at Tule Lake is climbing to upwards of eighteen thousand, with more arriving every day it seems.

Anyway, Mr. Kato just sent me in with the new arrivals and no one batted an eye. Once checked in, it didn't take me long to find my family and join them in their barracks. It took a long time for my mother to be able to look at me without crying!

Speaking of barracks, other than rocks and dirt, that's all you can see for what seems like miles: barracks after barracks. It is not a pretty sight.

I have met your friend Thomas and we have become great companions. And his sister is extremely attractive, I might add.

On another note, it is quite a shock to be here. For so long I struggled to get back to my home country, only to be treated like some sort of criminal. It is hard to believe. Where is the freedom and the rights I have always taken for granted? Of course, I don't blame you for any of this. You did all you could to help me get back to my family, and I appreciate it from the bottom of my heart. I look forward to the day I can thank you in person.

Say "Hi" to Stephan and Jeannie for me. And be

sure to give my love to Doc and Mrs. Dirksen.
Sincerely,
Brian Kikomoto

Jane felt a desire to be still and let the relief sink in. She went into Star's stall and sat in the deep straw, her back against the wall. Star stopped eating and lowered her head, blowing warm air into Jane's face. Jane smiled and rubbed the white hair that formed a star on the mare's forehead.

With energy renewed, Jane pushed herself up, gave Star a hug around her neck and went back to the saddle where she had placed the letters. She picked up the letter from Thomas.

May 16, 1943

Dear Jane,

Greetings from hot and miserable Tule Lake. I'm sure it is going to be the next vacation destination!

Brian is my one bright spot in this wretched place. He and I have become good friends, not to mention that he has a crush on my sister. He has a very nice family. I'm sure you would like them.

I have started helping my father in the kitchen. You know, I really am enjoying cooking, even in this heat. My father lets me experiment with new dishes. I think I have a knack for it. If I ever get out of here, maybe I'll look for a job as a chef.

Brian told me what you did for him. You are truly amazing. Send Jeannie my thanks for her help as well.

He also told me you are disguising yourself as a man and that you even fooled him. I laughed out loud when he told me that. You? A man? That must be some disguise. I don't know how you did it with such a pretty face.

Brian mentioned that you have a partner who is a great guy. I hope he isn't so great that he steals your heart!

Until we meet again,

Thomas

Jane smiled as she folded the letters and tucked them back in the envelope. In her next letter, she would need to tell Thomas all about Stephan.

37

February 1944

By the summer of 1943, fear of an invasion along the coasts had greatly diminished. The result was a reduction in beach patrols on both coasts and the Gulf of Mexico. The first patrols to be cut back in the autumn of 1943 were the dog patrols. Coast Guardsmen Smith and Wells, with whom Jane went on patrol while Stephan was recuperating, were withdrawn from Brookings and sent elsewhere. Jane didn't know where. Since Jane and Stephan were the only Coast Guardsmen in Brookings, they staggered their patrols. Sometimes they went out at night, other times during the day. They had become a familiar sight and the people of Brookings and the town of Harbor loved them just as much as the people in Lincoln City had.

The Widow Mullin, as she was called by all the townspeople, was very good at keeping Jane's secret, always introducing Jane as "John and his horse, Star." She also proved to be skilled at giving her "boys" haircuts, though she'd "tsk, tsk" as she cut Jane's blond curls and dyed the short hair brown. From the time Mrs. Mullin found out about Jane's true identity, she insisted that Jane move into her spare room in the house. "The barn's no place for a lady," she said. "And it's not proper for you to be in the same room with a man until you're married."

This made Jane blush, but she thanked Mrs. Mullin, and moved her belongings into the house.

"Hey, I'm a little jealous that you get the high-priced digs," Stephan said as he helped her move her things. Jane gave him a slap on the shoulder and smiled.

Day after day, Jane found herself struggling to control her fear for her brother Luke's safety. She wished she would hear from him. He was constantly in her prayers. Yet, no letters arrived from Luke. She did receive regular letters from Brian. In the letters, she picked up that Brian's spirits were as volatile as one might expect. In one letter he was optimistic about the future. In the next, he was consumed with anger at the situation in which he and the other Japanese American citizens found themselves.

With the news of the cutback in the beach patrols, Jane's concern was also for Stephan. If the

Coast Guard reduced the number of Sand Pounders, she worried that he might be sent to the Army or Navy.

Sure enough, on February 18, 1944, ADM Russell R. Waesche, commandant of the Coast Guard, announced a fifty percent reduction in beach patrol for the West Coast. The Army was going to return to many of the West Coast's beaches. The Coast Guardsmen were to continue to man beach lookouts and continue with traditional beach patrol activities, but the Sand Pounders were to be phased out.

Jane and Stephan received the news by way of a letter from their post commander. They were ordered to return to the Garibaldi Coast Guard Station on March 1st. There, they were to turn in not only their gear and tack but, in Stephan's case, his horse as well.

As Stephan read the letter, his face drained of color. Jane watched him. As soon as he was done reading, she snatched the letter from him.

She scanned through it before looking up at her partner. "Big Bay?" was all she could say.

Stephan stomped out the tack room door. Jane reread the letter. She rubbed her temples then followed Stephan to the area of the barn where the stalls were located. She found Stephan in Big Bay's stall.

Stephan was standing beside his horse, rubbing his horse's neck and whispering to him.

"What are we going to do?" Jane asked, hesitantly reaching out and touching his shoulder.

"Nothing we can do. He's not my horse. He belongs to the army," Stephan said, his back to Jane.

Jane's heart ached when she heard the tremor in his voice. She knew the horse belonged to the Army, but what would they do with him? During World War I, many American horses were shipped to Europe, never to return. But that wouldn't be the case now, would it? Surely the Army didn't need the horses for combat now that they used tanks and planes.

Jane went into Star's stall. The mare nickered. "Hi, girl," she whispered, cradling her soft muzzle in her hands. She couldn't imagine how hard it would be to lose her equine partner.

38

February 1944

A few days before they were set to leave Brookings, Jane received a disturbing letter from Thomas. Standing by the mailbox, she read:

January 29, 1944

Dear Jane,

I am sending this letter out with my father so you might notice the Klamath Falls postmark. I'm afraid that my letters are being censored by the camp personnel.

Things have become very difficult and even dangerous for me here. The already over-crowded Tule Lake camp has started receiving young Japanese men who are classified as "No-No Boys" and placing them in isolation.

Let me fill you in.

Our government, the very government that has put us in these concentration camps, has now decided that they need our bodies to go to war. Can you believe that? After depriving us of our civil rights and property, they want us to fight for our country. They gave me and the other young men around my age a "Loyalty Test." I must share with you two of the questions on the test.

Question #27 asked: "Are you willing to serve in the armed forces of the United States on combat duty, wherever ordered?"

Question #28 asked: "Will you swear unqualified allegiances to the United States of America and faithfully defend the United States from any or all attack by foreign or domestic forces, and forswear any form of allegiance or obedience to the Japanese emperor, or other foreign government, power or organization?"

Most of the adults in our barracks, and my father in particular, want me to agree in hopes that will prove our loyalty to the U.S. They actually expect me to say "Yes" to those questions.

Perhaps now you understand why the prisoners are called "No-No Boys." They are the ones who are brave enough to answer "No" to those two questions.

I had the chance to converse with one of the prisoners who had been brought here from the Heart Mountain camp in Wyoming. He told me that he, along with a half-dozen other internees at that camp, were so angered that their rights were being trampled on that they formed a committee to protest. They called themselves the Fair Play committee. Some of the members of the committee have been sent to Federal Prison. Others, like himself, have been shipped here and put in these prison cells.

Jane, I hope you will understand what I am about to tell you. I have decided to say "No" to those two questions. I am going to join with the "No-No Boys" in protest. I can't in good conscience fight for a government that has treated me and my family is such a terrible way.

Please know that I did not make this decision without much consideration. My biggest concern is for my family. Families of the "No-No Boys," (and there are some girls,) are being torn apart by this with one son enlisting and another refusing to enlist. The entire Japanese community at Tule Lake is also being divided and families are being ostracized. Some are even being denied attendance at our church services.

I hope you will understand and not turn against me, too.

Your friend and fellow American,

Thomas

Jane crumpled the letter in one hand and ran into Mrs. Mullin's house. Mrs. Mullin was in the kitchen and watched Jane run to her room.

Several hours later, Jane came out of the room. Feeding time had arrived and nothing could get in the way of caring for her horse, no matter the pain and sorrow she was suffering.

Mrs. Mullin noticed that Jane's eyes were red and puffy from crying. Her uniform was wrinkled.

"Jane, dear, what's the matter?" Mrs. Mullin said, drying her hands on the dishtowel and opening her arms.

Jane fell into them and buried herself in the warm hug offered by Mrs. Mullin.

Between sobs and stuttering breaths, she told Mrs. Mullin what the letter from Thomas contained.

Mrs. Mullin led her to a chair and offered her hot tea and a muffin. Then she sat beside her.

The kind woman patted Jane's hand and said, "War is a terrible thing, my dear. Rarely does any good come from it. Lives and families are destroyed. I'll not defend what our government has done to those poor people, but I have to have faith that all will work out in the end. Be strong for, and loyal to, your friend. Let him know you will be there for him. At this point, that is all you can do."

Jane looked down and picked at her muffin. She nodded her head. "Thank you, Mrs. Mullin."

39

March 1944

March 1st arrived crisp and clear . . . the kind of day that Western Oregonians see too rarely. Jane stepped out the back door of Mrs. Mullin's little house. She felt the sun warm her face and the cool, salty air fill her lungs. Regardless of what the day would bring, she had to smile as she hurried to the barn to feed.

While the horses ate their hay and grain, Jane and Stephan loaded the pickup with their gear and leftover feed. As Stephan organized their equipment in the back of the truck, Jane wrapped eight equine legs with travel bandages for the long drive. Stepping back and examining her work she was pleased. The wraps were neat and even, while not too tight or too loose. She didn't want another injury like Big Bay suffered before when trying to back out of the trailer.

She stepped out of Big Bay's stall and walked up to the truck. "Big Bay and Star are all set."

Stephan rested his hands on the side of the bed and forced a smile. "Thanks," was all he said. Jane noticed how dull his eyes looked.

"Do you want to come say goodbye to Mrs. Mullin with me?"

Stephan let out a long breath. "Sure. I guess. I'm not particularly good at goodbyes."

"I know. Me neither. But I'm worse at not saying them," she said with a smile and a pat on his hand.

They walked down the drive toward the Widow Mullin's house. Seeing no one around, Jane took hold of Stephan's hand. He clasped hers back as though needing a source of support. Mrs. Mullin had provided for them and their horses for nearly a year. It was going to be hard to say goodbye.

When they walked around the house to the front yard, Mrs. Mullin was standing on the porch holding a basket filled with sandwiches, fruit, and cookies . . . and carrots for the horses.

Jane started crying. Stephan cleared his throat as he blinked back the tears. Mrs. Mullin buried her face in her apron.

The drive up the coast was pleasant with few other vehicles on the road. The views along the coastal highway were spectacular. Jane never tired of watching the waves throw their might against the cliffs then roll peacefully up the sandy beaches. But even the beauty around them couldn't lift their spirits as they thought about Big Bay and what the future held for the wonderful horse.

Jane suggested they stop in Lincoln City to visit Doc and his wife and give the horses a break from the constant vibrations the animals had to endure while riding in the trailer.

Stephan nodded. "I'd like that," he said with a smile. "I'm sure the horses would like that, too."

Jane scooted over until she was sitting in the middle of the bench seat, pressed against him.

"Have you thought about what you want to do now that we won't be Sand Pounders anymore?" she asked.

"That's pretty much all I've been thinking about since the Commander sent us the letter," Stephan said, rubbing his hands back and forth over the steering wheel and frowning.

"I've been thinking about it, too."

Checking the rear-view mirror, he said, "And what have you decided?"

Jane looked over at him, noticing his jaw muscle twitch. "I'm going back to Tillamook. I want to be a girl again."

Stephan glanced over at her. "Jane, I want to talk to you about something."

Jane felt her heart pound and perspiration form on her forehead. "What is it?" The serious tone of his voice was unlike him.

"I don't quite know how to say it."

"Just tell me," she said, her voice catching in her throat.

"When this is all over . . . this war, I mean . . . I . . . well . . . I want us to make a life together."

Jane gasped; her hands flew to her mouth. For once in her life, she was at a loss for words. This was something she had not anticipated.

Stephan glanced over at her. "Am I being too presumptuous?"

"No. You are being marvelous," she said as she threw her arms around him.

Stephan smiled.

"Does this mean we're engaged?" Jane said, leaning back and looking at him, her eyebrows raised.

"Yes, I guess it does," he said with a chuckle and a twinkle in his eye that had been missing for the last month.

After visiting the Dirksens in Lincoln City, giving the horses a drink of water, and enjoying the lunch Mrs. Mullin had sent with them, the two Sand Pounders drove to Tillamook. They pulled into Jane's house and unloaded Star.

As his companion left him, Big Bay stomped and whinnied, but Star seemed to know right where she was. She pulled Jane down the unkempt road to the barn. Stephan tried to calm Big Bay by standing on the wheel covers and reaching into the trailer. He talked to his horse in soothing tones.

Jane got Star settled in her stall with some fresh hay and grain. She stepped out of the barn and stopped, placed her hands on her hips, and looked around. This was her home, the place she had grown up . . . her past. Just seeing it made her happy. Then she turned and looked up the drive to where she could see Stephan reaching in the trailer talking to Big Bay. That was her future and she smiled broadly.

40

March 1944

The Commander greeted the returning Sand Pounders warmly. Once horses were cared for and equipment and uniforms were turned in, the Commander held a meeting in the mess hall.

Jane was surprised at the large number of men, more than three times the number who had trained with her in August of 1942.

"Men, welcome back," he began. "It is a pleasure to address such wonderful and dedicated horsemen. Before I officially discharge all of you, I am going to make you sit through one more lecture from your Commander."

The Commander smiled and a chuckle flitted through the crowd.

He pulled out a piece of paper. "I hope you will forgive me. I had to write down some notes to make sure I had everything right and didn't leave anything out." He looked across the room and smiled again.

The Commander cleared his throat and started reading from his notes. "Horses have always been a part of the wartime experience, carrying men into battle since history has been recorded. Only recently has that changed, with the advent of tanks and airplanes in particular. But even those have not replaced the reliable horse completely. Even now, on the European front, a few horses are being employed to carry men and equipment to mountainous areas where vehicles cannot go. When the war escalated in Europe, the Army Quartermaster General for the Purchase of Horses, Mules, and Dogs, began purchasing horses and mules. In 1941 and 1942, the Army purchased 26,405 equines. Of that number, 3,222 were sent to the Coast Guard when it was decided that we would oversee the Beach Patrol.

"You men who stand before me were 50 of the thousands who answered the call to become Sand Pounders and protect our eastern and western coastlines. A few of you," and he glanced over at Jane, "even volunteered your own horses. Over 24,000 men, most of them horsemen like yourselves, were tasked with patrolling 3,700 miles of coastline, from Long Island to Florida, the Olympic Peninsula to California, and even the Gulf Coast.

"These wonderful horses not only allowed us to cover ground more quickly while carrying heavy equipment, but they also gave us greater visibility than we would have had on foot."

The Commander paused and Jane noticed his eyes blinking back tears.

He took a stuttering breath. "Now our job is winding down. By July only eight hundred Sand Pounders will remain on the West Coast, and none on the eastern shores. I know that many of you are disappointed that you didn't actually confront any enemy combatant trying to come ashore."

Jane and Stephan exchanged secretive glances at this comment.

"While we have not encountered any enemy invasions, you can hold your heads high. Who is to say that your very presence was not the reason the enemy chose not to come ashore? Without your diligence, we do not know what might have happened. The unknown cannot be measured. Nor can we measure the comfort you provided our own citizens living along the coast who felt so vulnerable and feared for their lives. I passionately believe that the very fact that no enemy invasion breached our borders is a certification of our complete success. Let me just say I am proud. Proud of the job you have done. Proud of the difficult circumstances you endured. Proud of the way you cared for your horses.

Proud of the way you represented the United States Coast Guard."

Applause broke out across the room. A few sailor caps were tossed in the air. Jane felt her heart swell with pride at being a part of this endeavor to protect and defend her country.

The Commander blew his nose before continuing. "Before I release you from duty, let us recite the Coast Guard Ethos one last time."

Every Sand Pounder in the room, stood up straight and tall. As one voice they spoke the words.

I am a Coast Guardsman.
I serve the people of the United States.
I will protect them.
I will defend them.
I will save them.
I am their shield.
For them I am Semper Paratus.
I live the Coast Guard core values.
I am proud to be a Coast Guardsman.
We are the United States Coast Guard.

"At ease men," the Commander said. Jane noticed that no one relaxed, including herself. There was too much excitement in the air to relax.

"Thank you. And now I want to give each of you an honorable discharge from the Coast Guard and thank you for your service. But before I do, are there any questions?"

Stephan tentatively raised his hand.

"Guardsman Peters?"

"Commander, Sir, what is to become of the horses?"

"Yes. I should have mentioned that. As we speak, a public announcement is going out over the airwaves and printed on bulletins and in newspapers. A public auction will be held at the fairgrounds in Tillamook on March 15th. Anyone is invited to bid on the horses. Each horse will go to the highest bidder."

41

March 1944

Jane jumped from the car before the engine quit rattling. She ran up the walkway that led to her grandmother's house. Stephan followed a short distance behind. On the porch, Jane took a deep breath, turned back and grinned at Stephan. "They are going to *LOVE* you," she said as he stepped up beside her. She locked one arm through his as she pounded on the door with the other.

The door opened slowly, and her Aunt Molly peeked out. As soon as she saw Jane, she let out a squeal, flung the door open, and threw her arms wide. Jane disengaged from Stephan and fairly flew herself into her aunt's embrace.

"My dear Jane," Aunt Molly sobbed.

"Aunt Molly," Jane responded, tears streaming down her cheeks.

Aunt Molly pushed back, her hands holding Jane's shoulders. "Let me look at you. What have you done to your hair?"

Jane shook her head. "It'll grow back."

Aunt Molly's eyes shifted from her niece to the young man standing, hat in hand, on the porch. "And who might this be?" she said, a twinkle in her eye.

"Aunt Molly, I'd like you to meet Stephan Peters. Stephan, please meet my aunt, Molly Morris."

Stephan stepped forward, his hand extended. "It is a pleasure to meet you, ma'am. I have heard so much about you."

"Might this be the man Jeannie told us about?" Aunt Molly said to Jane while not taking her eyes off Stephan.

"No doubt," Jane said with a laugh. "Aunt Molly, where's Grandma?"

"Oh. Of course. She will be thrilled that you have returned," Aunt Molly said. "She hasn't been feeling well lately. We'll need to go into her room."

Jane felt her heart sink, and her mouth dropped into a frown. "What is it? What's wrong?"

Aunt Molly patted Jane's hand. "Don't let yourself worry. Just old age, I'm sure."

Jane dashed across the living room, down the hall, and into her grandmother's bedroom.

"Grandma, Grandma, it's me, Jane," she said while shaking the sleeping woman.

Startled, Grandma Morris's eyes popped open. She shook her head in disbelief. "Do my eyes deceive me? Is this my little Jane?"

Jane leaned over the frail woman and hugged her. Placing her lips against her grandmother's ear she whispered, "I'm back."

Dinner was a lively event that night. Jane and Stephan shared story after story of their adventures over the past year and a half. Aunt Molly and Grandmother, who seemed to have regained her health just by being in Jane's presence, laughed and cried as they listened to all they were being told.

Talk eventually reverted to Luke and what little they had heard about the Pacific Theater. Grandmother and Molly had several letters from Luke, some addressed to them, others written to Jane. Molly reached behind her to the built-in china cabinet. On the top, within easy reach, was a stack of letters with a ribbon tied around them. She passed them across the table to Jane.

Jane felt a shiver run through her as she untied the ribbon and tore open the three letters addressed to her. Her hands trembled as she read each one. She saw that the postmarks on two of the letters were September and November of 1943, and the other was postmarked in January 1944. The letters gave her no information about where he was and what his duties were. They were, instead, a record of memories of his home and childhood that kept him going and hopes he had for the future. A flood of relief flowed through her as she realized that her beloved brother was alive at the time these letters were written. Her relief was quickly replaced with concern. *Is he still safe?* she wondered. *It has been two more months.* Each letter ended with, "Read your Bible and look at our picture. Whether you can see me or not, whether you can feel me or not, I'll always be beside you, holding your hand." A tear coursed down her cheek.

When the stories came to an end, Grandmother Morris turned to Stephan. "Tell me, young man, what are your intentions with my granddaughter?"

Stephan blushed.

"Oh Grandma!" Jane said, giggling.

"Well? I just want to know," she said.

"And you have every right to, Mrs. Morris. It is my intention to make Jane my wife if you will give me your permission."

"And how do you plan to support her?" Grandmother said.

Jane jumped in. "Stephan and I have talked about starting a riding academy and horse breeding facility. He was a champion show jumper before he volunteered for the Sand Pounders."

"Is there any money in that?" Grandmother asked.

Molly cleared her throat. "I'll be clearing the dishes now if you don't mind." She stood up and grabbed several plates before disappearing into the kitchen.

"Well," Grandmother repeated. "Is there?"

"I have my college degree and plan to work at a local bank until I have the money saved up to start the business. Then I intend to work with horses full-time."

"A college man? Well, that changes everything!" Grandmother exclaimed.

Jane locked her arm through Stephan's and rested her head on his shoulder. "I guess that's a 'yes,'" she said, smiling up at Stephan.

42

March 1944

People from as far away as Spokane, Washington pulled up to the fairgrounds in Tillamook. Others came from the Portland area, and still more came from up and down the coast. Many were pulling empty horse trailers. Some were there just to have something exciting to do. But most were there hoping to go home with a horse ridden by a Sand Pounder.

Jane was nervous as she and Jeannie found spots to sit on the bleachers. Her hand in her pocket fiddled with the thin roll of dollar bills hidden within. She had gone to the bank and withdrawn as much as she could afford — $151. She was sure that would be way more than enough.

"Can you believe how many people are here?" Jeannie said.

Jane shook her head. "I didn't expect this," she said before biting her lip and letting out a long breath of air.

"Do you recognize anyone?" Jeannie asked.

Jane looked over the crowd and was surprised to see several of the Sand Pounders, including Chip and Tim. With a floral print scarf over her head and red lipstick on her lips, she was sure they wouldn't recognize her. In any case, she was relieved that they were on the opposite side of the arena.

Right at the designated time, the first horse was led into the arena and the auctioneer started the bidding. "Fifty, do I hear fifty?" he shouted. Jane watched the horse, one she recognized from the time she was asked to test all the horses. Her heart ached as she looked in its worried eyes, its ears and tail twitching nervously. She wished she could run into the arena and comfort it.

The bids went up and soon the horse was sold. Jane watched as the lovely animal was led out of the arena and handed over to a young girl and an older man. Jane assumed it was a father and daughter, maybe the girl's first horse. The sight made Jane smile.

After several horses were sold, Jane saw Tim's palomino quarter horse being brought in. She watched Tim stand up in the bleachers across from her. When the auctioneer started the bidding, Tim's hand was the first to go up. Another man, just down the row from Jane, raised the bid. Jane looked down the row and examined the man carefully. He was an impeccably dressed gentleman, wearing an expensive-looking suit and a gray, wool fedora atop his head. On his hand was a large, gold ring. Jane had the impression that he could afford any horse he wanted.

Tim, still standing, raised his hand again. The man by Jane responded by calmly raising his hand, too. Tim removed his cowboy hat and wiped his brow before raising his hand again. The man sitting by Jane started to raise his hand for the third time. Jane jumped up. "Sir," she said, leaning across several people to get closer to him.

The man turned and looked at her, his hand pausing in mid-air. "Are you addressing me, young lady?" he asked politely.

Jane swallowed. "Sir, the man across the arena who is bidding against you is the Sand Pounder who has been this horse's companion for the last year and a half. Since he has donated his time to serve his country by protecting the coast, I doubt that he can afford to go any higher." She pursed her lips and pleaded with her eyes. The man, whose hand was already halfway up, looked at Jane. His face softened. He smiled, nodded, and dropped his hand.

"Sold," said the auctioneer.

"Thank you, sir," she said with a smile.

Jane turned and watched Tim crawl over the people in front of him. His face was lit in a bright smile as he jumped out of the bleachers and ran to claim his horse.

The afternoon seemed to drag on as Jane fingered the money in her pocket. She tapped her foot and fidgeted in her seat. At last, she saw Big Bay being led into the arena. His coat glistened, his long, black mane and tail flowed on the gentle breeze. An audible "Ohhhhh," echoed through the crowd. Jane's heart started pounding and the hand in her pocket began to sweat. With her other hand, she clasped Jeannie's arm. "That's him. That's Big Bay."

"I'm starting the bidding at $100. Do I hear $100?" shouted the auctioneer. Jane gasped. *Such a high starting price! Why such a high price?* she thought. She chewed on her lip.

Even at that high starting point, several hands shot into the air.

Jeannie turned toward Jane. "Aren't you going to bid on him?"

Jane clenched her jaw. Frozen in place, she watched the price rise. "$125, do I hear $130 for this magnificent horse? $130. Now who will give me $135?"

Jane felt her body tense as the price rose yet again to $140.

The auctioneer said, "$140 going once, going twice,"

Jane's hands formed fists, her short nails digging into the palms. She pulled her roll of bills from her pocket and jumped up. "$151," she shouted shaking the dollars in the air. The crowd around her became silent, all eyes on the young girl who had just bid the highest amount of the day.

Jane stared at the auctioneer, willing him to say the magic word.

"Sold!"

Jane collapsed back on her bench.

Jeannie squealed in delight. "You did it! You bought Stephan's horse!"

By the end of the day, the results of the sale of forty-nine horses at the Tillamook auction set the record for all the auctions around the whole country. The average price at the sale was $117 per horse. Big Bay's price served to raise the average.

That night, Stephan came to visit his fiancée. It had been a miserable day at the bank for him. His thoughts were constantly on the auction going on across town. He only hoped a kind person would be Big Bay's new owner.

Head down, he kicked at a rock as he walked up to Jane's door. He tapped on the screen. No response. He opened the screen and knocked harder on the door. No response. He turned the doorknob and opened the door. Inside, the house was dark. There were no sounds coming from any of the rooms. "Jane!" he called out, his chest tightening. "Jane, are you here?"

"I'm here."

Stephan jumped at the sound of her voice coming from behind him. He spun around. There, in the front yard, stood Jane holding the lead rope attached to Big Bay's halter. She extended her hand toward him. "Come take care of your horse," she said, a smile bigger than the moon across her face.

43

October 1945

May 8, 1945 marked the end of the war with Germany for the U.S. and Britain with the signing of an unconditional surrender by the new leader of the National Socialist party, Grossadmiral Karl Doenitz. Doenitz had replaced Adolf Hitler after the Fuhrer committed suicide on April 30th.

Celebrations broke out in cities and towns across America. Parades seemed to appear almost spontaneously. Cheering crowds of people, eager for the return of loved ones, lined the streets.

But Jane was not one of the ones celebrating. The war with Japan was still going on. That meant Luke would not be returning when the soldiers from Europe arrived home to welcoming arms over the course of the next four months. As happy as she felt for those families, the ache in her heart ran ever deeper.

Victory and surrender would not come easily for the Allies in the Pacific Theater. The war in the Pacific that had started with the Japanese bombing of Pearl Harbor in Hawaii on Dec. 7, 1941 was still going on.

Then August arrived and everything changed. After years of battles and unsuccessful attempts at negotiating a treaty, the United States dropped atomic bombs on Hiroshima and Nagasaki in early Aug. 1945. A week later, on Aug. 15, Japan announced its intention to surrender unconditionally. On September 2nd, General Douglas MacArthur accepted Japan's formal surrender aboard the U.S.S. Missouri, while anchored in Tokyo Bay.

A gusty wind blew the cap off the head of the tall, thin man as he trudged down the side of Highway 101. Clasping the pack on his back, he jogged across the road to retrieve it. Pushing the cap down on his forehead, he dropped his chin and continued south on the familiar road, a road he had not walked for more than three years. The rain came down in sheets as he turned onto the side road. His pack got heavier as it soaked up the water. His body shivered from the wet and cold. But none of this mattered. He was headed home.

He started jogging the last hundred yards or so and leaped up the front steps in a single bound. Clasping the doorknob, he didn't bother to knock. Throwing the door open he stepped into the warm shelter. "Jane, I'm home!"

The dinner plate Jane had been drying crashed to the floor. Trembling, she whirled around and dashed into the front room. With a squeal, she launched herself into the arms of her big brother.

Stephan arrived soon after. Grabbing her fiancé's hand, she turned to her brother. "Luke, this is Stephan. We have been waiting for your return to get married. I want you to walk me down the aisle."

Epilogue

In December of 1944, the U.S. Supreme Court ruled in favor of Mitsuye Endo in her case claiming that the forced incarceration of Japanese Americans was unconstitutional. After denying three previous cases with similar claims, this came as a welcome surprise to all the people of Japanese descent who were languishing in camps. It resulted in the release of inmates and the closure of camps during 1945 . . . with the exception of Tule Lake.

Jane became increasingly frustrated that Thomas and the Kato family, as well as Brian and his family, were still confined in the internment camp. Jane knew that the rest of the Kato family was applying to move to Denver where Mr. Kato had been offered the job of head chef at a historic hotel. Brian and his family were planning to go with the Kato family to Denver once they were released. The environment there was much friendlier to Japanese people as a result of Republican Governor Ralph Carr's efforts on their behalf.

But Thomas wanted to return to Tillamook.

Many people, even before the landmark decision by the Supreme Court, had applied through the Relocation Office to leave the camps. They were required to have a sponsor who promised to be responsible for them and provide them with work and a place to live.

In November 1945, Stephan and Jane, now the proud owners of a small stable set on twenty acres of lush pastureland and forest to the southeast of Tillamook, felt the time was right to appeal for Thomas' release. They had been discussing this for almost a year. But now that they were married and business owners, they felt they had a stronger case to make in Thomas's behalf. They filled out all the necessary paperwork required to sponsor him. The intent wasn't just altruistic. They found running the stable, teaching lessons, and training horses was a big job. They really did need the help. Additionally, they had a small apartment attached to the stable that Thomas could call home. It seemed the perfect solution. The application was sent in, and the waiting began.

On February 1, 1946, Jane went to the mailbox. A large envelope was stuffed inside. Wiggling and pulling, Jane was finally able to extricate the envelope from the box. Her eyes popped open, and she felt a shiver of excitement flow through her. In the upper left corner was printed the name and address of the Western Defense Command in Washington D.C. With shaking hands, she tore open the letter. Inside were the documents giving proper clearance for Thomas Kato to be released from the Tule Lake Interment Camp.

Just a few weeks before the Tule Lake Internment camp was finally closed in March of 1946, Thomas Kato arrived on the doorstep of Jane and Stephan's new home. He brought nothing but a grateful heart and a willingness to forgive. He made the commitment to himself that he would put the past behind and make this the beginning of a new life. He looked up at the sky and said a silent prayer of thanks, then raised his hand and knocked on the door.

Jane threw open the door. In her arms she held the Katos' kitty.

If you enjoyed this book, be sure to sign up for my newsletter. Don't worry, I promise I won't inundate you with frequent emails. I will just send you an update when I have a new release or some other exciting news.

As a gift to you for signing up for my newsletter, I will send you a FREE electronic copy of a short story based upon my

Award-Winning, bestselling novel:

"In the Heart of a Mustang."

Sign up by sending an email to: **mjevansbtm@gmail.com** and type "free gift" in the subject line.

Happy reading!

M.J. Evans

Bibliography

1. **Books:**
    a. Dressman, D and Elliff, J, 2018, *Beyond the Camps*, Vis-Op Publishing, Sterling, CO

    b. Noble, D, 1992 *The Beach Patrol and Corsair Fleet-The U.S. Coast Guard in World War II*, Coast Guard's Historian's Office, Washington, D.C.

    c. Reinike, L, 2018, *Football Flyboy*, Our House Publications, Littleton, CO

2. **Articles:**
    a. "Coast Guard 'Sand Pounders' Kept Oregon Coast Secure," Finn, J, Newport News Times, April 11, 2019

    b. "Mounted Beach Patrol: when the Service Saddled Up," Stephanie Young, August 12, 2012, Coast Guard Compass-The Official Blog of the U.S. Coast Guard.

    c. "Oregon History: World War II," Oregon Secretary of State website: sos.oregon.gov/blue-book

    d. "The Coastal Guardians," Horse Connection Magazine, April/May 2014

    e. "The Coast Guard at War – Beach Patrol XVII," 1945, Historical section, Public Relations Division, U.S. Coast Guard. Declassified.

    f. "The Sand Pounders: The U.S. coast Guard Mounted Patrol," Horses and History, November 19, 2014

    g. Walter, Anna, "1958, Office of the Quartermaster General,"   www.archives.gov

Acknowledgements

I am deeply grateful to Award-Winning Author, Denny Dressman, for his help with this book. He went through every chapter to make sure the historical elements were accurate. I could not have produced a quality book without his help.

The illustrations in this book were created by Hasitha Eranga and Gaspar Sabater. They were copied from actual photographs.

About the Author

Award-Winning, Best-Selling author, M.J. Evans grew up in Lake Oswego, Oregon, and graduated from Oregon State University. She spent five years teaching junior high and high school students before retiring to raise her five children. She is a life-long equestrian and enjoys competing in Dressage and riding in the beautiful Colorado Mountains.

You can connect with her on her website:

dancinghorsepress.com

Facebook:
https://www.facebook.com/margi.evans.98
Instagram:
https://www.instagram.com/mjevansbooks/

Pinterest:

https://www.pinterest.com/MJEvansFantasyNovelist

TEACHERS and HOME SCHOOLERS -
Visit the website for instructions on how you can
receive a FREE study guide:
www.dancinghorsepress.com

Additional Titles by M.J. Evans

The Mist Trilogy-Behind the Mist, Mists of Darkness, The Rising Mist
Gold medal from the Mom's Choice Award
First Place - Equus Film Festival

North Mystic
First Place – Purple Dragonfly Awards

In the Heart of a Mustang
First Place – Literary Classics Awards
First Place – Equus Film Festival
Second Place – Nautilus Awards
Second Place – Readers' Favorite Awards

The Centaur Chronicles- The Stone of Mercy, The Stone of Courage, The Stone of Integrity, The Stone of Wisdom

Gold, Silver and Bronze Medals – Feathered Quill

Silver Medal – Readers' Favorite Awards

Finalist – Book Excellence Award

First Place – Equus Film Festival

Purple Dragonfly Award

New Apple ebook award

PERCY –
The Racehorse Who Didn't Like to Run

First Place – Purple Dragonfly Award

Silver Medal – Feathered Quill Awards

Gold Medal – Literary Classics Book Awards

PINTO! Based Upon the True Story of the Longest Horseback Ride in History

First Place – Book Excellence Awards

First Place – Gertrude Warner Middle-Grade

First Place – Purple Dragonfly Awards

Plus seven other literary awards: Eric Hoffer Award, Readers' Favorite Award, American Fiction Award and more.

Mr. Figgletoes' Toy Emporium

First Place Feathered Quill Book Award

Finalist: Book Excellence Award

Finalist: Wishing Shelf Book Award (UK)

Winner: Purple Dragonfly Award

The Skullington Family Series: Boney Fingers, Bone Appetit, School is a Grave Mistake, Skeletons in the Closet

Readers' Favorite Five Star Award

Mom's Choice Gold Medal

Winner: Purple Dragonfly Award

Equestrian Trail Guidebooks:

Riding Colorado-
Day Trips from Denver with Your Horse
Riding Colorado II-
Day Trips from Denver with Your Horse
Riding Colorado III-
Day and Overnight Trips with Your Horse
Riding Colorado and Beyond-
Overnight Trips In and Around Colorado

All fiction titles are available on the Website: www.dancinghorsepress.com and wherever books are sold.

Made in United States
Orlando, FL
10 May 2024

46735602R00153